The Green Man

When fifteen-year-old O agrees to spend the summer with her ailing Aunt Emily, nothing can prepare her for what she is about to encounter. Emily, an eccentric poet and owner of the secondhand bookshop The Green Man, is haunted by unsettling dreams as long-buried memories of a magic show come back. While O works to bring order to the chaos of the shop and secretly begins to write poetry herself, she uncovers mysteries she cannot sweep away and falls beneath the spell of a strange boy, who may be more than he appears.

When the dark forces from Emily's past threaten to awaken once more, O is determined to discover the truth behind them while there is still time.

The Green Man

Michael Bedard

The
Green
Man

TUNDRA BOOKS

Paperback edition published by Tundra Books, 2014
Text copyright © 2012 by Michael Bedard

Published in Canada by Tundra Books,
a division of Random House of Canada Limited,
One Toronto Street, Suite 300, Toronto, Ontario M5C 2V6

Published in the United States by Tundra Books of Northern New York,
P.O. Box 1030, Plattsburgh, New York 12901

Library of Congress Control Number: 2011923467

Library and Archives Canada Cataloguing in Publication

Bédard, Michael, 1949-, author
    The green man / Michael Bedard.

ISBN 978-1-77049-511-1 (pbk.).—ISBN 978-1-77049-285-1 (bound)

    I. Title.

PS8553.E298G74 2012   jC813'.54   C2011-901448-3

Designed by Rachel Cooper
Cover illustrations: (bookcase) © Mark Graves, (open books)
© Elena Schweitzer, (girl) © Aleksandra Kovac, (ivy) © graph, (crow)
© Eric Isselee, (hand amulet) © Virginija Valatkiene, all Shutterstock.com

www.tundrabooks.com

Printed and bound in the United States of America

1 2 3 4 5 6   19 18 17 16 15 14

For you, Mom

ACKNOWLEDGMENTS

With many thanks to Susan Duff and Bob Knowlton for their insights into the world of the secondhand book dealer and for the generous gift of their time in reading and commenting on the manuscript.

I reckon – when I count at all –
First – Poets – Then the Sun –
Then Summer – Then the Heaven of God –
And then – the List is done –

EMILY DICKINSON

1

In the middle of the night the phone rang, wrenching O from a dead sleep. She lay listening through the thin wall as her father dragged himself from bed in the next room to answer it.

"Hello? . . . Oh, hello, Emily."

Emily was her father's older sister. She was a poet who ran a secondhand bookshop back East called the Green Man. One of the first books O remembered her father reading to her as a child was a collection of children's poems Aunt Emily had written. She still knew some of them by heart.

Her father said Aunt Emily was one of the finest poets of her generation. He kept copies of her books in a special place on the bookshelves that lined the living-room wall, along with a thin folder of reviews he'd clipped from newspapers and magazines over the years.

The books were few – five slim volumes of about fifty poems each, each book separated from the last by nearly ten years. That worked out to about five poems a year,

O figured, though her father assured her it was not quite as cut-and-dried as that. Instead, there would be sudden bursts of creativity, followed by long stretches of silence.

It was during the most recent stretch of silence that the late-night calls started to come. Father never complained about the time of the call. He just listened to her quietly, as he did now, assured her that things were not as dark as they seemed, and walked her back to the days when they were young and the world was new.

Eventually he calmed her down enough that she could go to sleep. Then he said good-bye, hung up the phone, and went back to bed himself.

Next morning, over breakfast, O asked about the call in the night.

"It was Emily," Father said, "going through one of her spells again."

"Why does she go through spells?"

"It's just part of who she is, O. Part of what makes her the poet she is."

Later that day, O took down the books and the tattered sheaf of reviews and looked through them again. The reviews were generally good, though more than one reviewer wondered at the thread of darkness that ran through her work. On the back of one of the early books was an old photo of her aunt – a thin, intense young woman, her long hair caught up in a bun, staring straight into the camera lens as if she could see down the decades to the girl who looked back.

It had been three years since O had last seen her aunt, at a rare family gathering one Christmas. With more than two thousand miles between them, and Father busy with his teaching and Aunt Emily with her bookshop, they saw one another infrequently. But there were always her cryptic letters in their spidery scrawl, and now the phone calls in the night.

Last fall, shortly before O's fifteenth birthday, a parcel arrived for her in the mail from Aunt Emily. It contained a secondhand copy of a collection of poetry called *A Treasury of Great Poems*. On the flyleaf of the book, her aunt had written *For Ophelia – Begin!*

Begin what? she wondered. It was yet another mystery in the many that surrounded her aunt. But the strange thing was, shortly after the book arrived, a number of things *did* begin.

First, early in December, they received word that Emily had suffered a mild heart attack. Endicotts had a history of heart disease – and a history of stubbornness to go along with it. Emily was kept in hospital overnight. The next morning, she checked herself out and went back to the flat above the bookshop, where she lived. She wouldn't hear of her brother dropping everything to come and take care of her.

Then, at the end of the winter term, Father received a grant to finish researching the book on the poet Ezra Pound he'd been writing for as long as O could remember. Ezra, slightly mad himself, was like a member of the family. The research would take her father to Italy for the summer. He invited O to go with him, but after the traumatic trip to Ireland they'd taken two years before, when the plane limped and lurched across the Atlantic on one engine, she refused to go anywhere near another plane.

So her father came up with a plan. He would go to Italy – and she would go to Emily. He called it "killing two birds with one stone." She, presumably, was one of the birds; Emily was the other; and he was the one with the stone. She felt he might have found another way of putting it.

Father wrote to Emily, explaining his dilemma and asking if O could possibly come and stay with her for the summer. If she said yes, which he hoped she would, it would also be a way of having O help Emily out – without her aunt suspecting it was part of his plan. Two birds, one stone.

After some delay, Emily wrote back. She seemed a little hesitant about the idea but, ultimately, she agreed. Father firmed up the dates with her over the phone, and it was settled.

But one last thing had begun since O received the book with its mysterious inscription. And, by mid-May, with the time of the trip barely a week away, it was this that led O to question her father a little more closely on the state of his sister's mental health, the morning after yet another middle-of-the-night phone call.

"Is Aunt Emily crazy?" she asked.

"We're all a little crazy in our own way," Father said. "Emily's a bit eccentric. Her axis is slightly off-center, so the world wobbles a little as it spins around her. She's a poet. Poets tend to be a little different than other people. Take Ezra, for instance."

"But is she a poet because she's eccentric, or is she eccentric because she's a poet?"

It was a fine distinction, but O had her reasons for asking. She wanted to know whether her aunt was crazy before she began to write poetry, or if writing poetry had made her that way. For the third thing that had happened since she received the book inscribed *Begin* was that she'd begun writing poetry herself.

For the time being, it was top secret – like some raging rash on an embarrassing part of your body. She hadn't breathed a word of it to anyone. But what she desperately needed to know was whether she had begun writing because she was another crazy Endicott, or if that was just a little something she could look forward to down the line.

"Emily's been the way she is for as long as I can remember," said her father, "always a poet, always a little odd.

I'm not sure which came first. I think maybe some people are just born to be poets, and there's not much they can do about it."

"Well, they could just *not* do it, couldn't they?"

"I suppose, but surely that could drive you crazy – not doing what you know in your heart of hearts you were meant to do."

"I see. So if you write, you go crazy. If you don't write, you go crazy. Wonderful."

Up to this point, her father had been only half-committed to the conversation. His eyes kept drifting back to the book he was reading. Now he put the book down on his lap and took off his glasses.

"What's this all about, O?"

"Nothing," she said.

He gave her that squinty-eyed look of his as he sucked on the arm of his glasses. She wondered if he suspected her secret. Recently, she'd been finding stray books of poetry scattered around the house like fallen leaves.

"Listen, O, Emily has a gift, a wonderful gift. But for every gift we're given, we're also handed an affliction. They're two sides of the same coin. Poets are not normal people. Normal people feel no need to write poetry. They're happy enough with the world as they find it and make the best of what life brings their way.

"Poets see through things . . . see behind things. They

6

remind us that the world is a much more mysterious place than we imagine. They're like explorers, bringing back news of unknown lands. Like most explorers, they're outsiders who don't quite fit. But if it weren't for the poets and the artists and all those other slightly eccentric people, there would be no one to remind us of the mystery. So we should be thankful for all those who are 'counter, original, spare, and strange,' as another crazy poet once put it."

That night, as she lay in bed trying to find the magic spell that would send her off to sleep, O thought of what her father had said about everyone being a little crazy in their own way. Some people might think her nightly ritual before bed was a little crazy – the way she had to arrange the things on her desk in a certain order, tuck the sheets in just so, tilt her mirror at exactly the right angle so as not to catch the reflection of the curtains, lock the closet door, and fold the quilt down carefully over the stuffed animals at the foot of the bed, so they wouldn't sit staring at her in the dark.

One night, simply to prove she wasn't a prisoner to the ritual, that it was silly and childish and slightly mad, she deliberately didn't arrange the things on her desk, didn't fold down the quilt in the proper way or tilt the mirror just so. She left the closet door unlocked and let the stuffed animals stare at her to their heart's content.

She didn't sleep a wink. The next night, she went back to doing things the way they were meant to be done.

O glanced at the clock. It was after twelve. She flicked on her light and took down A Treasury of Great Poems, hoping a little reading might send her off to sleep. The book was arranged chronologically. There was a brief biographical introduction to each poet, followed by a selection of his or her work. She had started at the beginning with Chaucer and was working her way slowly through. She was up to Andrew Marvell now, and so far there hadn't been so much as a whisper of madness.

She read until her eyes began to grow heavy. The stuffed monkey had managed to squirm out from under the quilt and was looking at her. She crawled to the foot of the bed and pulled the quilt over him. Before closing her book, she fanned to the front and read her aunt's cryptic inscription again.

"Begin," she whispered as she drifted off to sleep. "Begin."

2

Emily paced around the desk that stood in the center of the room. Round and round she went, as was her habit when the words would not come. Over time, her pacing had worn the rug around the desk almost bare. Some magic in the moonlight brought the pattern in the Persian carpet to life, so that as she passed through the band of light, she seemed to tread on a lush bed of luminous flowers and winding vines.

A swing-light with a dim bulb shone down on the typewriter that stood on the desk. Each time the circuit of the desk brought her back before the typewriter, she paused to glance at the sheet of paper it held, hoping to shake loose the next word . . . the next phrase . . . the next line in the poem that refused to be finished.

When words came, she sat down and added them to the rest, then began to pace again. Now and then she veered off course and stood by the window, staring into the night. Apart from the occasional car that whispered by, the street slept. There was something peaceful about the city at night, something calming in standing here surveying her estate.

She turned from the window and began her circuit of the room again. She let her mind prowl, pretending not to pay much attention to it. Her thoughts crept like a cat through the shadows, ready to pounce when the words showed themselves. The better part of writing was waiting.

As she paced, Emily recited the opening lines of the poem aloud:

> "The long dead come back
> Dressed in rags of dream.
> Eyes sealed in sleep
> Open wide again.
> Years slide away like stones
> Rolled back from mouths of tombs.
> The dead stride blinking
> Into blaze of noon."

As she rounded the desk, her eye fell on the corner of the envelope she had tucked under the typewriter. It was a letter from her brother Charles. She and Charles had kept up a correspondence that went back to when she had left home in her late teens and he was barely more than a boy. She had kept it all.

Over time, there had come a change in their relationship. Once, she had been the one offering comfort, especially during the dark months after his wife, Anne, had died, when Ophelia was not yet two. And then as he struggled to raise the child on his own, while establishing himself at the university.

But now, he was the one giving *her* advice. What had happened? Time had happened. And then there was the heart attack – just a minor one, the doctors assured her, but more than enough to send a shiver of mortality through her. Suddenly she was no longer invulnerable. Suddenly her mind was full of memories of her father, who had died of a similar attack while still a young man.

And now Charles was off to Italy for the summer to complete his study of Ezra Pound, and Ophelia was coming to stay with her. Emily suspected Charles had an ulterior motive for sending the girl to her. She suspected he was worried about his older sister and was seeing to it she had someone around to watch over her.

He had included a snapshot in his letter, a recent picture of Ophelia. She picked up the photo and studied it again. The girl, no longer a child, was a radiant young woman who stared boldly back at her. Her fair hair was short, her head cocked slightly to one side. Definitely an Endicott. She reminded Emily of how she herself had looked at that age – about the time when it had all begun.

And now it was poised to begin again. The thought filled her with dread. With the dread came the now-familiar tightening in her chest, the sudden knifepoint of pain, the feeling that she was unable to breathe.

She made her way over to the cot in the corner of the room and lay down. Fear washed over her in chill waves. She had been a strong woman once, but she was as weak as a kitten now. She closed her eyes. Just a few minutes rest and she would be fine. The lines of the poem spun round in her head:

> *The long dead come back*
> *Dressed in rags of dream.*
> *Eyes sealed in sleep*
> *Open wide again. . . .*

Sleep stole over her like a shadow. With it came the dream – the one that visited her almost nightly now. The dream of the magic show.

3

*T*he furniture in the room had been pushed back against the wall to make room for the evening's entertainment. It was a rare treat, and there was a thrill of excitement in the air. The children sat on the figured carpet before a makeshift stage that had been set up against one wall of the room. It was a hot August evening, and the tall bay windows had been thrown open. The curtains billowed lightly in the breeze, and the dim flames danced on the gas jets that had been turned down for the show, casting weird shadows on the walls.

A gilded table sat on the low platform that would serve as a stage. On it was a candelabrum and a box, about a foot square, decorated with Egyptian symbols. A full-length mirror stood to one side of the table and, on the other side, a low long wicker basket with a hinged lid. To the rear, a wrought-iron pedestal supported a brazier of coals that glowed in the shadows like a beating heart.

Darkness pooled at the fringes of the room, and while some of the children chattered among themselves, others of a more imaginative bent plumbed that darkness with wide eyes, wondering if something more than the dim shapes of armchairs and tables were gathered there.

"Look," cried one of the children, pointing to the shadows behind the stage. As all eyes turned that way, the darkness took shape and a tall lean figure strode forward onto the stage. As he approached the table, he snapped his fingers in the direction of the candelabrum. Instantly, the wicks atop the dozen candles danced with flame.

He stood silently in the candlelight and ran his eyes over the group of children seated on the carpet. Half a dozen parents and a serving maid stood uneasily by the door as his eyes drifted over them. He wore a black swallowtail coat over a stiff white shirt with a turndown collar, and a white cravat with a gleaming silver pin.

"Good evening," he said, as he slowly began to remove the white gloves he wore. "I am Professor Mephisto. And you are about to witness an evening of wonders such as you have never seen."

His voice was deep and melodious, and though he spoke quietly, the words reverberated off the walls like something echoing from the bottom of a well. His eyes glowed with a strange intensity and fixed on those who met them with such force that it was as if he could see into their very souls.

The children sat transfixed as he worked the gloves off his hands, one finger at a time. In the candlelight, his face appeared as pale as chalk, his lips as red as blood, his hair as dark as a raven's wing. He looked every bit a gentleman, yet there was something about him that sent a shiver down the spine.

The gloves removed, he tossed them into the air. And they were miraculously transformed into a pair of white doves. They swooped and circled the room, while the children craned their necks to follow their flight. Finally, they settled in the shadows at the rear of the stage.

"Now," said the magician, his eyes coming to rest on the parents gathered at the door, "it seems we have some very large children back there."

The children laughed as they turned to look. "Those aren't children!" one of them shouted. "They're parents."

"Parents? Really?" said the magician. "Well, that's very strange. I thought this was to be a children's show, was it not?"

"Yes!" shouted the children delightedly.

"Well, then, it seems we have two choices. Either we can ask the parents politely to leave, or, for my next trick, I could transform them all into children. Wouldn't that be a treat?"

"Yes!" shouted the children again, while the parents hung sheepishly by the door.

The magician lightly clapped his hands, and out from the shadows where the doves had disappeared flew two large black birds. They swooped menacingly low over the parents' heads. Finally, one of the adults opened the door and they filed out, glancing back nervously at the smiling figure onstage.

Then, with another light clap of his hands, the door shut with a resounding thud, the birds settled to either side of the stage, and, in the silence that followed, the show began. . . .

4

O found herself walking through a deep ravine. It was unlike any place she'd ever been, the vegetation so thick it was junglelike, the dense green canopy of trees all but shutting out the sun. She picked her way along the bank of a stream, scanning the shadows on either side for the presence she could feel lurking there.

"Caledon. Next stop, Caledon."

The voice came from a long way off, woven in with the distant drone of traffic in the dream. Someone touched her lightly on the arm, jolting her awake.

"Excuse me, Miss. I believe this is your stop." Opening her eyes, she saw the cute young steward with the French accent smiling down at her.

"Thanks," she said, quickly wiping away a trail of drool that had trickled down her chin and plucking the inflatable pillow from around her neck.

The traveler's pillow had been a going-away present from her father. It was designed to keep your head immobile while you slept sitting up. It came folded in its own little matching pouch. When you needed it, you simply blew it up like a beach toy until it took the shape of a giant donut with a big bite out of it. There was just one little drawback: you looked like a total idiot with it wrapped around your neck.

The first night on the train she'd resisted using it, but every time she drifted off, her head would snap forward and jolt her awake. By the time the second night rolled around, the trip had taken on a surreal quality, and she was more than ready for the traveler's pillow. She waited until everyone around her had passed out, then she took it out of its pouch and blew it up. Slipping it around her neck, she sat there feeling like a complete fool. But her head didn't bob as she began to drift off, and she dropped into an exhausted sleep that brought with it the strange dream of the ravine.

Now, half-awake, she fumbled her bag down from the rack above the seat. It was still dark outside, and everyone in the coach was sound asleep. She squeezed past stray limbs dangling into the aisle and retrieved her suit-case from the storage area at the rear of the car.

Caledon was definitely not a major tourist destination. No one else was getting off but her. The train screeched slowly to a halt. The sleepy-eyed conductor, his hat slightly askew, opened the door and put down the step.

As he was helping her down with her luggage, a voice called out behind her, "Excuse me, Miss." It was the cute young French steward, no doubt come to wish her a passionate good-bye. "You forgot this," he said and handed her the traveler's pillow she'd left on the seat.

"Thanks," she muttered, taking it from him and stepping down onto the deserted platform.

Twenty minutes dragged by. A halfhearted drizzle started up. She shuffled her suitcase and bag over to a bench under the wide overhang of the station roof, flipped open the valve on the traveler's pillow, and sat down on it to squeeze out the air. It made a sad whooshing sound that perfectly mirrored her mood. Clearly, Aunt Emily had forgotten she was coming, or Father had told her the wrong arrival time. Whatever the explanation, she had definitely been abandoned.

After walking the length of the wet platform, she made a quick circuit of the station building, just in case Aunt Emily might be waiting there. No sign of a living soul. The place had all the grim desolation of one of those *film noir* movies her father adored. It would have made a great place for a murder.

Soon the first rays of dawn began to brighten the sky. It didn't do the station any favors. As the darkness lifted, she saw weeds growing waist-high between the ties of a second set of tracks, on the far side of the platform. A rusty old luggage cart languished in the shadows at one end of the station building beside a broken vending machine. What had once been the waiting room was now a storage area, chock-full of railroad junk. The door was chained and padlocked, just in case rusty railroad junk was your thing.

The only part of the building still in service was a ticket window facing onto the platform close by the bench. A sign in the window said it was open between nine and five, three days a week. This wasn't one of those days. There was no rest room, no phone, no clock – nothing but the damp bench and the boarded building. *Welcome to Caledon!*

Someone called her name. For an instant it didn't register that it *was* her name, for apart from people who absolutely didn't know her, no one ever called her Ophelia anymore. People who knew her just called her O. It was a long story.

She turned to see a figure approaching from the far end of the platform, wearing a long loose trench coat, a broad-brimmed hat, and black rubber boots. Even before she glimpsed the familiar face peering out from under the floppy brim, she knew it could be no one but Aunt Emily.

"Ophelia," said her aunt as she hurried up to her. "Forgive me for being late. I'm afraid I dozed off. My,

I'd hardly know you! You've grown so." They greeted one another with a peck on the cheek and an awkward embrace.

"Where's your luggage?"

"Over there by the bench," said O.

They chatted as they walked with the luggage to the parking lot beside the station. There was only one car in the lot, an ancient station wagon that looked as if it had escaped from an automobile museum. Aunt Emily opened the rear door and lifted the heavy suitcase in with a grunt. She slid into the front seat and leaned over to lift the latch on the passenger side. With one fluid motion, she pitched a pile of books and papers from the passenger seat onto the backseat.

"There," she said, turning on the ignition as O climbed in. The ashtray was full of crumpled butts, and the car smelled of cigarette smoke. O rolled down her window. The smell of cigarettes made her sick. She got the window down about two inches, when the crank came off in her hand.

"Don't worry. That happens all the time," said her aunt as she put the car in gear and backed out of the space.

Soon they were creeping down the sleepy streets of Caledon. Her aunt drove hunched over the wheel, her eyes riveted to the road, as if she thought it might leap up unexpectedly and take a sudden twist. Reaching over with her free hand, she flicked on the car stereo, and the sound of jazz filled the interior of the car. O looked around for a place to put the window crank.

"Just leave it on the dash," said her aunt, with a sideways glance. "I'll take care of it later." A plastic statue of the Virgin, with a suction-cup base, was stuck to the dashboard. She surveyed the interior of the car with sad eyes and hands folded in prayer. It would take a good deal of praying to save this car, thought O, as she set the crank down beside the little lady.

While they were stopped at a light, Aunt Emily reached up and plucked off her hat. She sailed it into the backseat – where all unwanted things appeared to go. As she hummed along to the music, she tucked some stray hairs into the bun at the nape of her neck. O noticed there was a hollowness about her cheeks, slack pouches under her eyes, a general frailty that had not been there the last time she'd seen her.

She watched with alarm as her aunt fished a cigarette from a pack in her coat pocket and tucked it between her lips. "You don't mind if I smoke, do you?" It was more a statement than a question.

"Actually –" O started to say, but then the light changed and the car lurched into life, and somehow the words went unsaid.

"How's your father doing?"

"Fine. Getting ready to go to Italy."

"So I understand. Preparing to spill yet more ink on poor old Ezra Pound."

There didn't seem to be much to say to that. As the car filled with smoke, O glued her face to the window and sucked fresh air through the narrow gap. She was going to have to do something about this – and soon.

There was a tension to her aunt that she hadn't noticed when they met at the station – something in the set of her chin, the way her thin veined hands gripped the steering wheel as she drove. O had the strange feeling that she was not sitting with the Aunt Emily she remembered, but with some smaller, frailer, more fretful creature, who wore Aunt Emily's skin on her like an oversized sweater.

Something more than the smoke billowing through the car balled her stomach into a tight knot. She felt she might be sick.

"Are you all right?" asked her aunt as she turned onto a side street and began trolling for a parking space. "You look a little green around the gills."

"Stomach's just a bit queasy. I'll be fine once I get some sleep."

Aunt Emily stubbed out her cigarette and rolled down her window. The car cleared of smoke as the wind blew around the interior of the car, rustling the papers in the backseat.

For one crazy moment, O felt as if there were another passenger in the car with them, some infinitely fluid shape composing itself from the random papers rustling around behind them. At the same time, she saw Aunt Emily glance nervously in the rearview mirror.

"There's one!" cried her aunt as she swung the car into a free space at the side of the road. They climbed out of the car, and Aunt Emily hauled the suitcase out of the backseat. A very ordinary seat, cluttered with very ordinary books and papers.

"Push down the door latch and hold in the button on the handle while you close it," said her aunt. "Otherwise it won't lock."

They began walking along the deserted street. Aunt Emily lugged the suitcase, while O carried the bulging bag on her back. She hoped they didn't have far to walk.

When they got to the end of the block, Aunt Emily put down the suitcase, glanced up at the street sign, and muttered the names of the intersecting streets. She looked back to where the car was parked, then picked up the suitcase and begin walking again, still muttering.

She noticed O looking at her. "No, I'm not going mad. At least, no more than usual. It's just that, last week, I forgot where I'd parked the blasted car, and it took me an hour to find it."

O thought that losing the car might not be such a bad idea. "That suitcase is heavy," she said. "Let me carry it for a while."

"Actually, it *is* pretty heavy. It must be that gold brick you brought as a present for your dear aunt. You really shouldn't have. I'll tell you what, why don't we trade off? You take it for a block, and then I'll take it for a block."

They'd made the exchange twice, and there was still no sign of the bookshop. The strain of carrying the luggage had put an end to any small talk. They turned off the residential street and shuffled silently along a wide street lined with darkened storefronts. The occasional car slid by on silent wheels.

O was so tired, it was all she could do to put one foot in front of the other. It was like one of those dreams where you're trying desperately to move, but your feet feel rooted to the ground. She dragged them along for one more block, and then Aunt Emily stopped and set down the suitcase.

"Here we are," she said.

O glanced up and caught her first glimpse of the Green Man.

5

He leaned out from the old wooden sign like someone leaning from a window to look down at her. His green face was fissured with age, and the corners of his mouth were stretched wide by two thick green vines that sprang from them. The carved vines curled upward around his head and wound along the edge of the sign, until they met below and branched into the letters that spelled the name of the shop – The Green Man.

The sign swayed in the wind. As it swayed, it creaked. To O's sleepy mind, the creaking sounded like an ancient voice, struggling to speak. She stood transfixed beneath the sign while Aunt Emily searched for her keys.

O had never seen anything like it before. What could such a strange thing mean? she wondered. It frightened and yet fascinated her. There was something deeply human in the grotesque figure, something that touched her despite the green stalks spilling from his mouth.

It was almost as if he were trying to tell her something.

She stared up into the ancient face, trying to make out words in the creaking voice.

"I see you've met my friend."

O jumped about a foot in the air.

"Sorry. Didn't mean to startle you," said her aunt, looking up at the sign. "It was he who first drew me into this shop. I look on him as a sort of guardian spirit, watching over me.

"There," she said as she opened the door. "Welcome to the Green Man."

Even in the faint light of day, there seemed something magical about the shop. It was as if it had wandered from a different time and place and set itself down here, on a street corner in Caledon.

O picked up her suitcase and hauled it inside. The smell of dust and old books greeted her as she stood in the deep shadows just inside the door, while her aunt wandered off to turn on the lights.

"Don't move," Aunt Emily warned her. Then the lights came on and O saw why.

Books were everywhere. The outer walls were lined with shelves of them from floor to ceiling. Two freestanding ranges of books ran the length of the shop, each of them six feet high and crowned with spires of still more books. The two ranges divided the shop into three narrow aisles, one running down the center and two along the sides.

The narrow aisles were made narrower still by box upon box of books stacked at the base of the shelves along each aisle. Some of the boxes were open, their loose flaps like vines launching across a tenuous jungle path, threatening to reclaim it as part of itself. Others had split like ripe pods and spilled their contents onto the floor.

Aunt Emily flicked on another light at the rear of the shop, revealing even more unpacked boxes ranged around an enormous wooden desk, crowned with precarious piles of books.

O could see now what the Green Man was trying to tell her in his creaky, vine-choked voice: "Turn around, girl. Go home! You *don't* want to go in there."

She picked up the suitcase and threaded her way down the center aisle, toward the back of the shop.

"Things have gotten a little out of hand," said her aunt sheepishly, as they stood and looked back at the chaos of the shop. "Don't tell your father."

Turning from the desk, she walked toward the book-lined wall beside it. She reached up under a shelf, and, as if by magic, a door swung open in the wall of books, revealing a narrow set of stairs that launched up steeply to the second floor.

Aunt Emily flicked a light switch. Nothing happened. "Can you manage that suitcase by yourself?" she called back over her shoulder as she started up the stairs.

Drifts of books were piled at the sides of stairs all the way up – books in the process of making their way up or down. Halfway up, her aunt sidestepped one of the stairs.

"Must you always sit on the steps?" she muttered.

"Pardon me?"

"Oh, not you, my dear. It's Mallarmé. He insists on sitting on the stairs. Not a thing I can do about it."

There was no one there, but O sidestepped the stair anyway.

Aunt Emily opened the door at the head of the stairs, and they entered a kitchen. A lean white cat was up on the table, licking milk from the bottom of a cereal bowl. It took one look at the stranger, launched off the table, and disappeared down a hall.

"That's Psycho," said Aunt Emily. "It will quickly become clear why she has that name."

The state of the kitchen was a variation on the theme established downstairs. There was clutter everywhere. The only things that looked in place were the dustpan and broom that hung from a hook inside the door. It appeared as though they hadn't been taken down for some time.

They crossed the kitchen and started up another flight of steps. If she had to haul this suitcase up one more flight, thought O, she would be the one having the next heart attack.

The stairs deposited them before a door on a dim landing, with no more stairs in sight. Aunt Emily reached up and took a key down from the ledge above the door.

"When I first moved here, this was where I used to write," said her aunt. "I use it mostly for storage now." She turned the key in the lock and pushed open the door. They stepped inside.

"I'm afraid it's a little musty. I'll open the window and air it out a bit."

O set down her suitcase and looked around. So this was what she'd traveled two and half days through train hell for! She could have cried. It was the saddest-looking room she'd ever seen. The low ceiling sloped sharply to one side. A folded cot stood in a corner, covered in plastic sheeting. Other pieces of furniture hid beneath drapings of white cloth. A dozen boxes were scattered over the dusty floor, with the inevitable books piled on them.

After a bit of a struggle, Aunt Emily opened the window and a breeze blew into the room. The drapings on the furniture rustled like woken ghosts. The covers of a few stray paperbacks fluttered open, flapping their mute tongues.

"Nothing a little tidying won't cure," said her aunt. "I'll go fetch a broom and some rags." And off she went, leaving O rooted to the spot, unable to imagine turning the room into anything livable.

—

Over the next hour, working together, they shifted the boxes over against one wall, swept the floor, removed the plastic sheeting and opened out the cot. They slipped the white drapings from the furniture, uncovering a large old dresser with a mirror, an elaborately carved bookcase – miraculously empty – and a cherrywood secretary desk with a matching chair.

"This desk belonged to my grandfather," said Aunt Emily, lowering the leaf to dust inside. "It was passed on to me when he died. I first began to write while sitting at this desk – long ago and far away.

"Now, I'm sure we can find some curtains for that window. The door beside it leads to a little deck outside. I used to sit there in the warm weather and sun myself. It has a nice view of the neighborhood. Just don't wander too close to the edge. It's quite a drop."

Off she went again and returned a few minutes later, carrying a bundle of bedsheets, a pillow, and a pair of red brocade curtains. Standing on the chair, Aunt Emily hung the curtains. To O, it felt like a piece of a puzzle falling into place, and she wondered if these curtains had hung here when her aunt used the room.

They made the bed together, tucking the corners in securely, spreading the sheet and blanket, and plumping the pillow.

"There," said Aunt Emily. "I'll leave you to yourself

now. I'm sure you must be exhausted. The bathroom's downstairs, along the hall. And if you're hungry, you know where the kitchen is."

"Thanks. I think I'll just get some sleep."

"Good. I'll see you when you get up, then." Her aunt looked as if she was about to say something else. But then she turned and left the room, quietly closing the door behind her.

O sat down on the edge of the bed. There was no doubt about it; the woman was a little strange. She thought about unpacking her suitcase into the dresser drawers, putting her few books on a shelf of the bookcase, tucking her journal and sheaf of poems away in the drawer of the secretary. She thought about putting on her pajamas.

Instead, she lay back on the bed. She heard the drone of traffic in the distance, the opening and closing of doors and drawers as Emily moved about in the kitchen below. The bedsprings groaned beneath her.

The curtains, patterned with a repeating motif of roses, glowed red against the light. As the breeze blew through the open window, it gently rustled the roses. They seemed to drift through space. O felt herself drifting with them.

Suddenly the room seemed filled with their scent. As she teetered on the edge of sleep, O felt a little flutter of unease. But it was only a flutter, and, in an instant, she was asleep.

6

O sat at the kitchen table, washing down a peanut butter sandwich on stale rye bread with mouthfuls of strong black tea. It was a little after noon, according to the clock that hung on the wall over the stove. She had woken up ten minutes earlier to the delicious aroma of baking bread and stumbled downstairs drooling, only to be informed by her aunt that the smell came from the bakery next door.

O loathed peanut butter sandwiches, but it was either that or starve. A peek in the cupboards had revealed an exhaustive range of dried beans in dusty jars – and not much else.

The fridge sat in the corner of the room, humming to itself and trying to look busy. There was next to nothing in it either, and what there was looked highly suspect.

"Maybe I could do a little shopping," she suggested as she choked down another mouthful of the sandwich with a swig of scalding tea. It felt like she was getting second-degree burns on her throat.

"Oh," said Aunt Emily, as if this was a startling new idea. "Yes, I suppose we could use a little shopping. There's a health-food store a few blocks up the street."

"I was thinking more of a supermarket."

"A supermarket?" Obviously a new word in her vocabulary. "I imagine you'll need some money."

"Yes. That would be good."

It was like talking to someone from a distant planet – not hostile, just a little vague about life on Earth.

"There's money in the tin on top of the fridge," said her aunt.

"Thanks. I'll think I'll go and unpack first."

Back upstairs, O took her clothes from the suitcase, flattened out the wrinkles as best she could, and tucked them away in the dresser. She angled the dresser mirror so she could see herself in it. Placing A Treasury of Great Poems on the top shelf of the bookcase, she took her journal and sheaf of poems to the desk. She opened the journal and read what her father had written on the first page: To my darling O – May your words bloom and bear fruit among the leaves of this little book. Love always, Dad.

The sight of his handwriting called up the sound of his voice, and for a moment, he was there in the room. Her hand went instinctively to the small silver pendant he had given her for her last birthday. Shaped like a hand, it was minutely engraved on both sides with mysterious words and symbols. As she held it now, she felt like she was holding him.

Turning to the last entry she'd made in the journal, she decided to sit down and write a brief account of the train trip while it was still fresh in her mind. When she was finished, she tucked the book away in the desk and turned her attention to the boxes. Aunt Emily had said she was free to go through them. They might contain some pic- tures and ornaments she could use to decorate the room.

It was a glorious day. The first hint of summer was in the air. Rather than sit inside, O decided to haul the boxes out into the light to see what they contained.

The rooftop deck was about eight feet square, bounded by a low brick wall just high enough that you could easily stumble over it and plummet straight to the ground, twenty feet below. In one corner, a metal railing inter- rupted the wall at the entrance to a rusty fire escape that snaked down the side of the building. A dingy plastic table and two matching chairs sat on the sun-bleached boards near the window. Drifts of dead leaves had gath- ered at the base of the wall beneath it.

O carried a box outside, set it down on the table, and began to go through it. It was full of papers – notebooks, sheaves of yellowed typescript, drafts of poems on random scraps of paper bundled with string. There were packets of old letters and postcards, some of them dating back almost fifty years. She fanned through them and found several from her father. She wondered if he knew his sister had kept them all this time.

One by one, she went through the boxes, unearthing several treasures – a clutch of paperweights wrapped in faded tissue paper and nested side by side in a shoebox, a pair of ivory elephants crossing an ivory bridge, and several delicate watercolors in worn wooden frames. She set them all aside.

There was one box left on the floor of her room. Her aunt called up the stairs to say she was heading down to open up the shop for the afternoon. O unfolded the flaps and took a peek inside. This box was different. It contained a wealth of old family photos – school pictures of her father and Aunt Emily and their siblings; photos of family vacations, Christmases, and birthdays. With the rest of the family scattered around the continent, it seemed to have fallen to Aunt Emily to be the keeper of the family history.

As O was sifting through the photos, she came upon one of a woman in white, her long hair parted in the center and a string of beads about her neck. She was smiling into the camera. It was her mother on her wedding day. She and her dad had met at a poetry reading when they were in their twenties. He said that, when she read, it was as if a crystal dome had settled over the room. And when she spoke into the stillness, it was as though the words were being born.

Some people lead epic lives, long and full. Some lead lyric lives, short and too soon over. Her mother led a lyric life. She died of leukemia before she was forty. O was just a toddler at the time. Her memories of her mother were gleaned from faded snapshots in old photo albums.

She hauled the box out onto the porch, where she could study its contents more closely in the light. As she was lifting it onto the table, something caught her eye. The short street that ran beside the shop dead-ended in a high stone wall. A boy was sitting astride the wall, looking at her.

He was a fair distance away, and it was hard to see him very well, but there was something eerily familiar about him. She set the box of old family photos down. They looked at one another for what felt like a long time but was probably no more than a few moments. Then the boy swung his leg over the wall and dropped out of sight.

7

A few minutes before O's experience on the rooftop, Emily was making her way down the dim stairs to open the shop after the lunch break, the cashbox tucked under one arm and a mug of hot tea in her hand. She did her best to dodge the books heaped at the sides of the stairs, while keeping one eye on the steaming tea, which threatened to slop over the edge of the mug.

The stairs were liberally spotted with milky tea stains from many a day's descent to the shop. In her younger years, she had been a better housekeeper, but recently such minor mishaps occurred somewhere on the fringes of consciousness and were quickly forgotten.

So, too, with the books that accumulated unchecked on the edges of the spotty stairs. She navigated around them as though they were a permanent feature of the landscape. Occasionally, she would see the steps for the disaster they were and resolve to tidy them before she took a tumble down them one day and broke her fool neck. But then the thought would slop over the edge of her mind, as the steaming tea slopped over the lip of the mug onto the dusty stairs, and be forgotten.

At the foot of the stairs, there was a light in the ceiling, which could be turned on by a switch at either end of the staircase. The light did not work – not because it was broken, but simply because the bulb had burned out several months back and had suffered the same fate as the drifts of books and the tea spills.

It was age, Emily told herself in her more anxious moments. Age, which would send her shuffling down increasingly narrow passageways, through increasingly dim rooms, until she dropped at last into a narrow pit from which she would never clamber out. A poetic thought, though a trifle grim. Most of her thoughts these days were grim.

That, too, was age. She hardly had a thought now that was not stamped by time, like those pathetic cartons of food in the fridge that lingered on beyond their expiry dates, which she picked up, eyed skeptically, sniffed, and returned untouched to the shelf.

She was not the woman she once was, and *that* was the lamentable truth. What she would give for one crisp, clear, unclouded moment – one moment that would enfold her and whisper sweet words in her ear. Poetry was made of such moments – not this whimpering nonsense that went endlessly round in her head, like the painted horses on a merry-go-round.

Bah! she said to herself as she pushed open the door to the shop with the toe of her shoe. She put the tea down on the edge of the desk, slid the cashbox into the top drawer, and shook a cigarette from the open pack she kept there. She fished the lighter from the pocket of the sweater she wore, lit the cigarette, inhaled deeply, and blew smoke into the shadows of the room.

It was a bad habit, as her doctor never failed to inform her, and a dangerous one for someone in her condition, whatever *that* was supposed to mean. But it was a habit that went back to the time she had first started down the winding road that led to here, and she was not about to let it go.

She took another drag and set the cigarette down on the edge of the ashtray that occupied part of the precious bare space on top of the large oak desk. Switching on the desk lamp, she ambled over to fetch the pile of books she'd bought yesterday morning from Miles.

Miles MacIntyre was one of a dying breed – the book scout. He made regular rounds of the Goodwill and Salvation Army shops during the week; spent Saturday mornings trolling the streets for promising yard sales; stood hours in line to get first pick of the books at church-basement rummage sales and at the university book sales in the fall; ran ads in the local papers saying he was looking for book collections; and had an uncanny nose for estate sales, where private libraries often surfaced. Among "pickers," he was without peer, always on the lookout for books he could buy at a bargain price and resell to a dealer for a profit.

He used to move like clockwork from one secondhand dealer to another, trundling his boxes of books from the trunk of his beat-up car into shop after shop and making a decent living. But now, many of the dealers had closed their doors, and those who were left had more stock than they could handle. Book scouts, like book dealers, were an endangered species. Those who remained, like Miles and herself, were simply too stubborn or stupid or set in their ways to let it go.

And so every Friday morning, she would sit at the desk and wait for Miles to drive up to the front of the shop in his rusted-out old beater and come walking through the door with a box of his latest finds. While she sifted through them, he'd pop into Gigi's next door and pick up two large double-doubles and an almond croissant to share. Then the two of them would spend the better part of an hour talking shop – trading news of other dealers in town and how they were doing or not doing. Who was reeling under the latest hike in rents; who had decided to fold his tent and take his business onto the Net; what sales were coming up and what they might find there; what was happening with the out-of-town sales.

They'd sip their coffee down to the sugary syrup that coated the bottom and do their best to raise old ghosts and ignore the new ghosts that dogged both their days. And, at the end of it, she'd buy most of the books in his box, even though she didn't really need them – more for the sake of giving him something to tide him through the week, until they came together again. Two old prospectors, panning for gold on the same old river they had worked for years, still dreaming of the big find – a treasure trove of wonderful old volumes only they knew the true value of, which would end their financial worries forever.

Emily took the books she'd bought yesterday from the box and carried them to the desk, where she would clean them up, price them, and distribute them around the shop. She set them down, took a final drag of her cigarette, and butted it out. She would open the window by the desk a crack to air the place out, then flip the sign in the front door and open for the afternoon. A little later opening than usual, she glanced toward the front door to see if anyone was waiting.

There *was* someone standing at the front window, peering in, not at the display of books in the window, but at her. Their eyes met – and she gasped in shock.

The figure stood on the shade of the awning, backlit by the bright sunlight, but still she recognized him instantly. It was her brother Charles, Ophelia's father. Not Charles as he looked now, but as he had appeared as a boy. The shape of the face, his short fair hair, those unmistakable eyes staring back at her now with the same sense of shock that she looked at him.

Everything felt unreal, as insubstantial as a dream. She gripped the edge of the desk, as much to assure herself it was solid as to steady herself. Her hand trembled as she reached for her glasses, suspended from a cord around her neck, and slipped them on.

She looked at him again and saw now that he was sweating from the heat. She let go of the desk and walked toward him, her legs trembling. Each step she took through the shadow-hung shop was a step back through time. By the time she reached him, she would have sloughed off this ridiculous old body and become the young woman she had been then.

But she had taken hardly half a dozen steps before he suddenly turned from the window and, with a glance back in her direction, took hold of a bundle buggy by his side and walked quickly away.

Charles! she cried somewhere deep inside her. Hurrying through the shop, she fumbled open the door and looked desperately down the street. He was not there. The gap in time that had delivered him to her had closed, leaving only a bewildered old woman staring down an empty street, with an ache in her heart and a fear in her bones she had not felt for many years.

"Hello, Emily." It was Gigi from the bakery next door, sweeping the sidewalk in front of her shop. "Lovely day, isn't it? Summer will be here before you know it."

"Yes," said Emily. "Lovely." She rearranged some of the sun-bleached books in the shallow bargain bins out front, flipped the sign in the door, and retreated back into the shop.

Outside, the Green Man hung from his perch above the street. The carved leaves that curled from the vines spilling from his mouth shivered lightly in the breeze, and his ancient all-seeing eyes watched a boy with a bundle buggy turn hurriedly down a side street and disappear.

Inside, Emily switched on the lights in the shop. She went to the desk, sat down, and took a small bottle of pills from her sweater pocket. Shaking one of the tiny pills into her palm, she tucked it under her tongue. The vice around her chest loosened slowly as the pill went to work.

She glanced up at the calendar on the wall beside the desk and felt the dark wing of fear brush her cheek as it flew by.

8

When O came downstairs into the shop, she noticed the smell of cigarette smoke. Aunt Emily was sitting at the desk.

"I was thinking I might do that shopping now," she said. Her aunt looked up at her with wide, startled eyes.

"Are you feeling all right?" said O. "You look a little – I don't know – spooked."

"Just lost in thought," said her aunt, with a weak attempt at a smile.

"I was wondering if you had a bundle buggy – for the shopping?"

"A bundle buggy? Yes, there's a buggy out back."

"Are you sure you're okay?"

"I'm fine. Did you find the money?"

"Yes, I took some from the tin on the fridge."

"It's probably easier to take the buggy out the back way rather than try to bring it through the shop."

"Fine. I shouldn't be long."

"Be careful," her aunt called after her.

It was one of those things her father would automatically say when she was leaving the house, but coming from Aunt Emily, it took on a slightly different tone – as if there might actually *be* things to be careful about.

Beyond the desk, a partition divided the shop in two – the larger room out front and, behind it, a second, smaller room. Here, too, the walls were lined with bookcases, and boxes were ranged along the floor at their base.

The room was large enough to accommodate an old stuffed couch, a tattered armchair, and a small wooden table covered in coffee rings. A number of folding chairs were nestled together against the back wall, on a small raised platform covered in worn carpeting. O wondered what they could be for.

The room seemed to be one of Psycho's haunts. Cat hair clung to the dark fabric of the couch, and the upholstery along one side of the armchair had been raked by claws. Under the table were a bowl of water and a dish of dried food; a litter box was tucked between two boxes of books, just inside the doorway. There was no sign of Psycho.

"I can't seem to see that buggy," called O after a quick look around the room.

"It must be on the porch – through that red door in the corner," called Aunt Emily.

The ramshackle wooden porch had been added on to the original building. It was crammed with flattened cardboard boxes, some parceled together with string, but most apparently pitched in at random. The buggy hung from a nail on the wall alongside an ancient ladder. O waded through the sea of boxes and lifted it down.

She wrestled open the bolt on an old wooden door and found herself in the small yard she had seen from the upstairs deck. The distance had done it favors.

The yard showed signs of having been something once. It wasn't much of anything anymore. The grass grew wild, and weeds sprang between the flat stones laid in a wavering line from the building to the tumbledown garage. The garden was a graveyard of dead flowers. Here and there, a perennial poked its head from the ground and unfurled a hopeful flag of color, despite the bleak surroundings.

Against the back wall of the building stood a wooden stoop to reach the slack clothesline that ran between the building and the garage.

O bumped the buggy down into the yard. To her left, a high wooden fence hid it from the street. To the right, an ancient fence was trying to maintain the property line between the Green Man and the bakery next door. A fan rattled in the back wall of the bakery and poured the enticing aroma of baking bread into the air.

When O had looked down at the garden from her perch on the deck, what she'd taken for a large white stone proved to be a piece of sculpture – the face of a girl, lying in the earth, looking up at the sky. It was made of plaster and was, no doubt, meant to hang on a wall. From lying in the garden, the features had become weathered and worn. In time, she imagined, they would wear away altogether.

As O bent over her, the girl in the garden seemed to stare back. For a moment, she felt that if she leaned close enough to those parted lips, the girl would whisper in her ear all the secrets spoken by the dead beneath the soil.

O wheeled the buggy over to the gate in the high fence, lifted the latch, and went out. Instead of turning to the left toward the shops, she turned right and started down the dead-end street she had seen from the rooftop.

The buggy creaked behind her as she walked. The street looked different than it had from her perch on the roof. Where she was sure there had been a row of bungalows, there was now a duplex. Where there had been a tall old tree, there was now a parking pad. By the time she reached the wall, she was no longer sure it was the same street at all.

O turned and looked up at the rooftop deck of the Green Man. There was no doubt – this was the place she had seen the disturbingly familiar boy. But things had subtly changed.

She wheeled the buggy back up the street and began her search for a supermarket. She passed the health-food store her aunt had talked about and, a couple of blocks further along, came across a nice family grocery business – two aisles, fresh fruits and vegetables. The woman on cash didn't seem to mind being paid in small bills and change. She even helped O load the bundle buggy with her purchases.

As she wheeled the buggy back to the shop, O got a sense of the neighborhood. It was a neighborhood in transition. There were businesses that had been there for a long time – a pool hall, a shoe repair, a hardware store, a clothing store with its ancient mannequins posed in its dowdy windows, and a small family restaurant frozen in time. Most of them could have used a fresh coat of paint, but they seemed to scrape by. The Green Man fell into this category.

But alongside them were new businesses – antique shops, corner cafés, home-décor places, and tech shops. Old and new eyed one another suspiciously.

O sensed that, if they could, they would wrench themselves up by the foundations and drag themselves over to where they wanted to be. All the old shops would huddle together for mutual support, and the new would band together for strength. Now they sat side by side, like strangers on a train.

As she approached the Green Man, O looked with a different eye at the tall elegant windows and the ornamented woodwork. It was looking a little tired, but the Green Man was still a grand old shop.

For the second time that day, she stood beneath the elaborately carved sign that overhung the street. The Green Man looked back at her, his forehead furrowed, his face encircled in leaves.

He made his little creaking sounds as he rocked back and forth in the wind. Again it seemed that he was trying to talk. But all that came out were leaves and branches.

The incident of the boy on the wall had all but passed from her mind. It might have stayed that way had it not been for something Aunt Emily said at dinner that night.

·

9

The cupboard was full of – imagine it – *food*! The fridge was full of – wonder of wonders – *food*! The buggy was back on its nail on the porch; the sauce was simmering on the stove; the water was boiling for pasta; and there was garlic bread in the oven. All was right with the world.

O knew how to cook. It had been a simple matter of survival. Growing up with just Father and her at home, making dinner for the two of them had become her job as soon as she was old enough to be trusted not to burn the house down.

It had taken her some time today to get used to the unfamiliar kitchen, to find where everything was, to figure out exactly how the gas stove worked.

Twenty minutes ago, Aunt Emily had come to the bottom of the stairs in the shop and called up, "What on earth are you doing up there? It smells delicious." Now she was tucking into her second plateful of spaghetti. "Your father said nothing about your being such a wonderful cook," she said. "I haven't eaten this well in ages. I used to be a pretty good cook myself, when I was younger. It's hard to keep it up when you live alone."

A question formed in O's mind. She wasn't sure whether to ask it or not. "Why did you never get married, Aunt Emily?"

Silence. Her aunt looked down at her plate.

"I'm sorry," said O, blushing. "It's really none of my business."

"Don't be silly. It's a very good question. I'm just not sure I have a good answer. When I was your age, I would never in my wildest dreams have imagined I wouldn't marry. What can I say? Things happen – things you never expected. Life takes turns, and you go with them.

"At about the time most people start thinking about getting married, I was beginning to write. I poured everything I had into that. Then I went away to school, and afterwards I traveled – by car, all over the country – with a suitcase crammed with clothes and a backseat full of poems. I just wrote them and pitched them back there. Lord knows how many poems I lost that way! It didn't matter. I felt that as long as I hung on to the poet, the poetry would come.

"Now and then, I'd gather the best of them together and send them off to a small press I knew that specialized in poetry. They liked my work, and a couple of those early collections were published. I took what jobs I could, where I could find them, but none of them were what I really wanted to do. I wanted to roam and write poems, like Kerouac and Corso and all the other vagabond poets I'd read about.

"When you're constantly on the move, it's hard to get to know people well. The time just slipped by. I guess poetry was my guy. We've been together a long time – though we don't talk much anymore." She took a piece of garlic bread and mopped up the sauce on her plate.

"Now don't follow my example, you hear me? You don't want to waste your culinary skills on yourself. But there's little danger of that. I'm sure a pretty girl like you is beating off the boys."

"I wish. I'm not even allowed to date yet."

"Well, I'm sure your father's just looking to do what's best for you. He's a good man. He's certainly cared for me over the years. If it hadn't been for him, I wouldn't have this place."

O gave her a puzzled look.

"So he never told you about that. Well, it's true. Twenty-eight years ago, after having been away for a long time, I came back to Caledon. There was something I had to take care of. Once that was done, I didn't feel like moving around anymore. I wanted to set roots down in one place – this place.

"One day I was out walking, wondering what I was going to do with the rest of my life, and I found myself on this street. I looked up, saw that sign, and – well, now you're going to think I'm a bit mad – it spoke to me somehow. I stood at the window awhile . . . and then I went in and looked around, and I discovered two of the little books I had loosed upon the wind sitting on the shelf in the poetry section. I plucked up the courage to introduce myself to the owner, and he recognized my name. I can't tell you what a wonderful feeling that was!

"I fell in love with the place. Pretty soon I was dropping by almost every day and got to know the owner quite well. He was a poet himself, a grand old creature from another era. He believed in poetry strongly enough that he shed his kindly influence on all who came near.

"It was a quiet shop even then. So he was glad for the company, and I was eager to learn everything I could about the business. I knew I had found my home.

"Well, things went on like that for a couple of years, and then, one day, he let it slip that he was thinking of retiring and was going to have to put the place up for sale. He asked if I might be interested. I jumped at the opportunity. I had already been working for some time in the shop by then and had learned quite a bit about the business. When I look back on it now, I see that he'd had his eye on me as his successor and had been quietly teaching me what I'd need to know for some time.

"Unfortunately, I hadn't any money to speak of. *That* hasn't changed. I tried to get a bank loan, but they turned me down flat. Poets, it seems, are poor credit risks.

"Your father had already moved out West by then. I talked to him on the phone and told him about the offer to buy the shop. He asked the name of the place, and, when I told him, he asked me if it was in the west end – a corner shop with a carved sign. When I said yes, without so much as a pause he offered to loan me the money for the down payment.

"He said he thought it was my destiny to have this shop. Now 'destiny' is a mighty big word, and it struck me as a strange thing for him to say. But I guess he was right. It *has* been my destiny. Over the years, this shop and I have come to fit together like hand and glove. It's the best thing that ever happened to me. And I owe it all to your dear father. So that's the story. Except –" She poured herself a cup of tea.

"What?"

"You'll think I'm crazy."

"No, I won't."

"I saw him today."

"Who?"

"Your father. I was opening the shop after lunch, and I saw him standing outside."

"That's impossible. Dad's in Italy."

"All the same, I saw him. Not as he is now, but as he was as a boy."

O felt the hairs on the back of her neck rise.

"He was standing outside the shop, looking at me through the window. When I walked toward him, he turned away. And by the time I got outside, he'd gone." She picked up her tea and wandered off into the living room.

"You must be mistaken," said O, feeling a sense of unreality wash over her.

"No, it was him, all right. I'd know that boy anywhere." She set her tea on the edge of the book-cluttered coffee table and sat down.

"What was he wearing?" O heard herself ask.

"Well, you know, that was very odd. It looked like a pajama top."

"Long sleeves, with blue cuffs and collar," O heard herself say.

Her aunt stared at her. "That's right. How do you know?"

"After you went down to the shop, I was out on the deck going through one of the boxes from my room. I noticed a boy sitting on the wall at the end of the dead-end street, looking back at me. That's what he was wearing. There was something familiar about him. But it can't have been Dad. It was just someone who looked like he did back then."

"I suppose," said Aunt Emily, sipping her tea, letting the silence wash over them. "Of course, there is another possibility."

"What do you mean?"

"We live in the midst of mysteries, my dear. They surround us on all sides, and, for the most part, we take no notice of them. Take Time, for instance. What is it? Where does it come from? Where does it go?"

She leaned forward and took a book from one of the piles on the table. "Imagine that this book is that very small piece of reality we call the present – you and I, here, now." She stood it between two tall piles. "This moment stands between a future that is not yet real and a past that is no longer real." She placed her hands on top of the piles to either side. "Before we know it, it too has slid into the past, and another moment has come to take its place.

"But what if it is not as simple as that? What if all those past moments still exist, as real as the books on this pile, but hidden from the present moment by a thin fabric, like the painted backdrop in a play? Say that in certain places that fabric were to wear thin and tear, and what lay on the other side were to spill out? Perhaps they would be places where the pressure of the past had grown so great that it could no longer be contained.

"Maybe the Charles I saw at the window spilled over from the past. Maybe he *did* once stand at that window, walk down that street, sit on that wall as he did today. And if a boy with a buggy could slip through, perhaps other things could cross over in the same way."

It was clear she was no longer talking to O, but to herself. The words hung in the air, like the smoke in the closed car.

Aunt Emily stood up. "I think I'll go heat up this tea."

Nothing more was said of the matter, but for the rest of the evening O found her eye drifting repeatedly to the book propped between the two piles on the cluttered coffee table.

Time was hard to keep track of at the Green Man. One day flowed seamlessly into the next. Before she knew it, they had turned the calendars to June, and the weather was heating up. Their lives had fallen swiftly into a pattern. They ate breakfast together, then went down and opened the shop a little after ten.

Since her "incident," Aunt Emily had taken to closing the shop for an hour at noon to eat and rest a little before reopening. But after O had been there two weeks and had begun to learn her way around the shop a little, she abandoned the practice. She started leaving O alone while she went upstairs, assuring her that, if anything came up, she was just a shout away.

Most days, they closed a little before six. After dinner,

they read and listened to Aunt Emily's jazz collection and chatted the evening away.

O noticed things about her aunt that reminded her of her father: the way she held her head to one side when she listened to you, the infectious laugh that bubbled up from somewhere deep inside her when something struck her funny.

Despite their difference in age, she found she was quite comfortable with her aunt. But, then, Aunt Emily was not your normal adult. There was still a lot of the child about her. Maybe that was what made her a poet.

One evening as they sat together, O took a book from the top of one of the piles – a collection of Chinese poetry translated into English. She started reading and was quickly captivated by the simplicity of the words, the clarity of the images, the deep emotion that pulsed below the tranquil surface of the poems.

When she glanced up, Aunt Emily was snoring in her chair. Her glasses had slid to the end of her nose, and her book lay slack in her hands. As O sat looking at her, the words of a poem came into her mind. She grabbed a pencil and a scrap of paper and quickly wrote them down:

Sleep steals quietly into the room.
Eyes grow leaden and close like flowers.
Books grow drowsy on the shelves.

If you listen, you can hear
The murmur of dreams in the still air.

As she crept quietly from the room, she heard her aunt moan softly in her sleep.

10

The magician performed tricks with cups and balls, sleights of hand with handkerchiefs and linking rings. Reaching into the wicker trunk, he brought out a pair of intricately wrought mechanical birds, which flapped their jewel-encrusted wings and sang on command. Next he withdrew the miniature figure of a man in Hindu costume, sitting cross-legged on a small decorated box. The automaton was less than two feet tall. He asked several volunteers up onto the stage to examine it. They were invited to ask the figure mathematical questions, which the automaton answered by reaching into a hatch beneath his left hand and sliding numbers in front of a small opening.

The mechanical man was also able to play cards with them. The magician dealt the cards and placed those the automaton was dealt in an arc-shaped holder before him. The mechanical man selected the card he wished to play by swinging his arm up, plucking the card from the holder, and showing it to the audience. He won every game he played.

"And now," said the magician as he tucked the figure away, "we have come to the entertainment entitled the Mystic Mirror. I will need a volunteer from the audience." He rolled the large mirror forward to the front of the stage. It was set in a heavily ornamented wooden frame, with a pattern of leaves and branches skillfully worked in the wood. Here and there, the hint of a face peered through the leaves.

When the magician had asked for volunteers before, he'd given each of them a copy of a little book, which he said contained the secrets of his magic art. Several children clutched copies in their laps. But now there was a hesitation, for it suddenly seemed to the children that there was something oddly mechanical about the magician himself, as if behind the veil of flesh were only cogs and wheels and bloodless moving parts.

"Come, come," said the magician in his soothing voice. "I assure you, there is nothing whatever to fear. Surely you have all wondered what lies within the mirror's depths. Is the world we see there the same as this? Is it simply an illusion, or can we enter the mirror world and return to tell the tale? Come now, I need one brave spirit, an adventurer in the realm of magic."

His deep eyes settled on a boy who sat among the others. Without a word, the boy rose and approached the stage.

"Let's give this brave young man a hand," said the magician. He walked the boy over to the mirror, where he stood facing his reflection in the glass.

"Now I want you to reach out and touch the surface of the

mirror," said the magician. The boy reached out and touched the glass.

"How does it feel?"

"Cold," said the boy.

"Indeed. Then perhaps the mirror world is a colder world than ours. You must go prepared." He reached into the wicker trunk and took out a heavy cloak. He laid it over the boy's shoulders and drew its deep hood over his head.

"Now, this time, I want you to reach out as if you were laying your hand on the handle of a door. Give that handle a turn and walk through. Are you ready?"

From within the depths of the hood, the boy nodded his head. An uneasy silence fell over the room.

As the boy reached out his hand again, something rose from the flat surface of the mirror to meet it. The boy's hand closed over it. He gave it a twist and strode forward.

A gasp went up from the crowd as first his arm and then his entire body slowly passed through the surface of the mirror. The cloak fell in an empty heap to the floor. One of the younger children screamed.

Like the surface of a pool after someone has plunged in, the mirror settled into stillness again. Once more, the trappings of the stage were reflected in its calm.

"Who knows what wonders await us on the far side of the mirror," the magician said. "Perhaps our brave adventurer will tell the tale."

He turned, and from the deep shadows behind the stage, the boy walked forward. The magician pressed a copy of his little book into his hand. To the applause of the crowd, the boy took his place again among the others.

But as the show continued, several children seated nearby noticed a strange chill in the air about him and shifted nervously away.

11

Emily took a long look in the dusty mirror mounted on the wall by the desk. She reached out, put her hand to the glass, and gave a little push, as if she half-expected it to go through.

The radio, tuned to the local jazz station, sat humming to itself on the shelf beside the desk. The desk was piled high with books and papers. The papers on the bottom had been there so long, they had begun to turn color. It was a vast sea of chaos, with a tiny island of order directly in front of her, at which she worked.

Today, she was making her way through a box of books she'd bought from a young man who had come in that morning. She needed more books like she needed another hole in her head. But she had a soft heart, and when some poor soul came through the door with a box of books for sale, she was as likely as not to buy the lot. Meanwhile, O was busy dusting, muttering to herself about the condition of the shop, just loud enough to be heard.

Over time, a bookshop will take the shape of its owner. Emily had been at the Green Man so long that it had grown around her like a second skin. The books were her flesh; the words that flowed through them were the blood that ran through her veins. The poetry section was the beating heart of the collection. Along with the familiar names, it contained many scarce and obscure items – small-press publications, chapbooks, broadsides, limited runs, books by local authors.

But the mazy aisles and teeming shelves of the shop mirrored other interests in her life as well. Just inside the doorway to the back room were three shelves of books on Victorian stage magic. And on the wall of books that ran the length of the shop beside the desk was a full bay devoted to supernatural fiction.

The supernatural collection was a large and, in many ways, a private collection. Much of it was housed along the hallway of the flat above the shop. It was, without doubt, the most valuable part of her entire stock, and she guarded it zealously, keeping the full extent of it secret from all but her closest friends.

The roots of her interest in the supernatural ran deep. Now and then, one of the shop regulars would gently scold her about it. "You don't really believe in all this bunk, do you?" Emily would arch her eyebrow, as she did when something got her goat, and her brow would furrow lightly.

For the supernatural was not something she merely dabbled in; she was deadly serious about it. She herself had experienced incursions from that realm just the other side of what people liked to call the "real" world, and those incidents had shaped her into the person she was.

As with all the serious things in her life, she wrapped her beliefs securely in silence. Wasn't that the poet's task, after all – to safeguard the silence? It was not merely the words on the page that mattered, but what one glimpsed from time to time through the latticework of letters.

She was a friend of silence, an ally of the dark. She had always done her most creative work at night, while the rest of the world slept. She needed the silence so that she could hear her own words forming; needed the dark so that she could see her own small light burning. She caught sleep when she could.

Lately, sleep held its terrors. Twice in the past week she had dreamt the old dream. It had been years since she'd dreamt in that terrifying way – blissful years, they seemed to her now.

The sun was warm on her back as she sat at the cluttered desk, prepping books before adding them to the stock. She sprayed a little watered-down Windex on a cloth and wiped down the covers of the paperbacks until they gleamed.

The radio was playing an old Bix Beiderbecke number, "Singin' the Blues." Pure poetry. Beiderbecke had the sweetest tone of any horn player she had ever heard. She let the tune wash over her as she fanned through the books, checking for markings, seeing if the past owners had left anything behind.

People left the most remarkable things in books: postcards, pressed flowers, photographs, locks of hair, love letters, newspaper clippings, theater tickets tucked away for safekeeping and then forgotten. Bits of life, left unknowingly behind.

The books she was working on now were all fairly new and yielded nothing but a scattering of light pencil markings, which she carefully erased. She dipped into several of the books as she readied them for the shelves. It was one of the pleasures of the job, and a necessity, she assured herself. For she needed to know a little about the items she was adding to the collection. Up until recently, she had personally shelved every book herself. That way she knew exactly where everything was. Now, things had changed.

Since her "incident," as people politely called her heart attack of a few months back, she had been unable to do many of the chores around the shop she had before. She was not supposed to lift anything heavy, not supposed to stretch and strain. The slightest overexertion or upset brought on an attack of angina and resort to the tiny nitroglycerin pills she had to tuck under her tongue, where they quickly dissolved and took away the pain.

Until now, she had managed quite well with the aches and pains growing older had sent her way. But this was different. There was an unmistakable smell of mortality about the pain that visited her now. And her doctor pulled no punches in letting her know that, if she was not careful, she would be bound for the secondhand bookshop in the sky sooner than she might imagine.

As much as she resented her independence suddenly being taken from her, she knew in her heart of hearts it was a godsend that Charles had found some excuse – transparent though it might be – for sending Ophelia to spend the summer with her. She was a very bright girl, with a good sense of humor and a nice keen edge to her. Emily would not be at all surprised if what Charles suspected about her was true.

Emily gathered up the books she had gone through and was about to call Ophelia to shelve them for her.

"Oph –" she began, and quickly stopped herself, remembering the exchange at breakfast that morning.

Ophelia had prepared oatmeal. It had been years since Emily had eaten oatmeal. Normally, a quick coffee and a cigarette were what she used to ease into the day. But the oatmeal was Ophelia's way of seeing that she started on a more heart-healthy diet. The girl was on a mission.

Emily sat down at the table, poured her coffee, and went to light up a cigarette.

"I'd rather you didn't do that."

"Excuse me?"

"I said I'd rather you didn't do that." Cool as a cucumber. She'd done some odd thing with her hair. It looked like she'd stuck it in a socket.

"But I always have a cigarette with my morning coffee."

"Well, it's not good for you. And I *know* it's not good for me. So I'd rather you didn't." And with that, bold as brass, she snatched up the ashtray from the table, emptied it in the garbage, and put it in the sink, running water in it.

Emily was left holding the book of matches in her hand, the unlit cigarette dangling from her mouth. It was *her* house and she wasn't about to let this slip of a thing with the electric hair – she saw now that there were red streaks running through it – tell her what she could or couldn't do in it.

She yanked a match loose from the book. Testing the limits, that's what they used to call this back when she was the eldest in a family of little demons who were always seeing exactly how far they could go. She brought the match close to the striker.

"Don't . . . light . . . that," said Ophelia, turning from the cupboard, where she was searching for something or other.

She folded her arms across her chest. Plucky young thing. She gave Emily a look that was pure Charles – Charles with electric hair. Was that eyeliner she was wearing?

Emily looked right back at her, the match poised over the striker. The nerve of the girl. The cheek, as her grandmother used to say. Yield now, and there would be no stopping it. She lit the match.

"Don't," warned Ophelia, as if she were talking to a child. "It makes me feel sick. It makes my clothes stink. Oh, and – by the way – it will kill *you*! Do you have any brown sugar in this place?" She turned back to the cupboard and started going through tins.

Emily sat holding the match while the flame crept perilously close to her fingers. Finally she blew it out, perched it on the edge of the table, plucked the unlit cigarette from her mouth, and put it back in the pack. The entire incident had about it the unmistakable odor of defeat. She would live to fight another day, she assured herself, as she pushed the pack of cigarettes into her dressing-gown pocket.

The brown-sugar search finally yielded results – an opened package in a tin in a corner of the cupboard. Emily had no idea how long it had been there. She could not remember having bought it. It had fossilized in the package – a solid brown rock of what had once been sugar. Ophelia chipped away at it with a grapefruit spoon until there were enough shards to scatter on their oatmeal. She wrote *brown sugar* down on a scrap of paper and taped it to the spice shelf above the sink. Not only was the girl a tyrant; she was an organized tyrant.

The oatmeal was delicious. But Emily sulked – justifiably, she felt – and said nothing. Still, when offered seconds, she readily accepted. Ophelia went at the brown sugar again with the grapefruit spoon.

"That's not necessary, Ophelia."

"Please don't call me that." She was chipping with a passion now.

"Call you what?"

"Ophelia."

"Well, that *is* your name, isn't it?"

"Yes," she said, plunking the oatmeal down in front of Emily, "but none of my friends call me that."

"Why ever not?"

"Well . . . let's see. How about because it's a perfectly hideous name? How would you like to be named after some girl who goes mad and drowns in a river? No, wait – drowns in a river, singing?"

"As you wish. But don't you think you're being a little hard on the poor girl? Consider her situation. She's in love with Hamlet, and he is in love with her. Her father forces her to betray him. Hamlet goes mad, rejects her, and kills her father. The weight of all that grief and guilt is too much for her to bear, and she goes mad. She's not the first to go mad from heartbreak – nor, I suspect, will she be the last."

Ophelia was mining brown sugar for her oatmeal and appeared to be paying not the least attention.

"Very well, then," said Emily. "What *do* I call you?"

"O."

"O?"

"Yes. O."

"You're kidding?"

"I've never been more serious in my life. My name is O. Not Ophelia, not Oph, not Felia. Just O."

"And that's what your father calls you?"

She nodded.

"Very well, then, O it is – on one condition."

O looked over at her.

"That you just call me Emily. Not *Aunt* Emily. I *detest* 'Aunt Emily.' Just Emily. Deal?"

"Deal."

So now, as she gathered up the books for Ophelia to shelve, she corrected herself. "O, I have another few books here for you to shelve."

She found she actually liked the quirky sound of the name. It suited the girl. Perhaps she should start to call herself E.

Then again, maybe not.

12

LITERATURE – front room, right wall, alphabetical by Author. MYSTERIES – front room, left wall near window, alphabetical by Author. PHOTOGRAPHY – front room, right aisle, shelves facing PSYCHOLOGY.

And how did you spend your summer, O? Well, actually I had an absolutely amazing summer memorizing the Subject Guide to the Green Man bookshop. I know, I know. Guess I just happened to be in the right place at the right time.

O flipped the page: POETRY – front room, center aisle, left side, just past CHILDREN'S BOOKS.

She walked the aisles with the list in one hand and a pink feather duster in the other, locating each section as she read it off the list. They were identified by hand-lettered cardboard labels, thumbtacked to the shelf. She ran her eye over the contents of each section, pulling out a title or two that caught her interest, running the feather duster over the tops and the spines of the books.

If the shop had a mouth, it would have laughed at the feather duster. The shop was way beyond feather-duster stage. Dust lay thick over everything. What they really needed was a huge vacuum cleaner – or a small hurricane. All the duster did was stir the stew around a little.

O ran her eye over the contents of the poetry section. She recognized some of the "biggies," like Keats, Coleridge, Wordsworth, Whitman, and Eliot, but many she'd never heard of before. There were even a couple of Emily's books tucked among the masters. She pulled out one and looked at the black-and-white photo on the back cover. A very young Emily looked back. There was a touch of the otherworldly about her even then. It seemed she was not so much looking *at* you, as *through* you.

She was suddenly aware of Emily staring at her from the desk. Sliding the book back in place, she moved on. The last thing she needed was to show that she had an interest in poetry. That was her secret, and she intended to keep it that way until she was ready.

That morning, she had tangled with Emily over her smoking. It wasn't like her to lash out like that, particularly at an adult. It had been the fatigue talking.

In the three weeks she'd been at the Green Man, O had gotten into the habit of leaving the door at the foot of the stairs to her room open a little at night. She wasn't exactly afraid of being alone up there, but she'd heard noises – noises she couldn't put a name to. They'd start up as soon as the house was still. It was probably nothing more sinister than mice moving in the walls or raccoons scampering across the roof. But her imagination had different ideas.

Last night she'd gone to bed, as usual, with her copy of *A Treasury of Great Poems*. She had made her way safely through the seventeenth century without so much as a mention of madness. But as she entered the eighteenth century, all that changed.

It was the Age of Reason. Poetry was considered a decorative art. Those poets who dared search for deeper truths were scorned. Isolated and ignored, they did the one thing any sane person would do – they went mad.

Suddenly mad poets were everywhere – William Collins, William Cowper, Christopher Smart, William Blake. An epidemic of madness. Christopher Smart composed his long poem *Song to David* while confined in a madhouse. Denied the use of pen and paper, he scratched the verses on the walls of his room with a key.

William Blake claimed to be in communion with the spirit world. He spoke in a matter-of-fact way of the spirits of dead poets who visited him and inspired his own poems. He said everybody had the ability to experience visions and simply lost it through neglect. Most people thought he was mad, and he lived in poverty and obscurity for most of his life. Despite that, he wrote some of the most beautiful lyrics in the English language.

O drifted off to sleep while she was reading. She wasn't sure how long she'd been sleeping, when suddenly she woke with a start, her heart pounding. There was a smell of roses in the room. Could it have drifted up from the back garden? she wondered. Or had Emily crept into her room to check on her while she slept and left a lingering scent of perfume behind?

She fumbled for the lamp by the bed and switched it on. The book was lying on the floor. The sound of it falling must have woken her. She lay back against the pillow, trying to calm herself.

Then she began to hear the noises again. They sounded like footsteps, moving stealthily around on the deck outside her room. She thought of the fire escape snaking up the side of the building and wondered if someone had stolen up it. She had the terrifying feeling that if she went to the window and threw back the curtain, she would find someone staring at her through the glass.

She lay awake for ages, too afraid to go and see if there actually was someone there, too afraid to fall asleep in case there was. Finally she got up and carried the boxes that had come with the room over in front of the door to the deck, stacking them six high and two deep. No one would be coming through there now without her knowing.

It was nearly four in the morning before she calmed down enough to close her eyes. Immediately she dropped into a dead sleep.

So when O stumbled downstairs that morning, she hadn't been in the best of moods. Which explained the blowup at the breakfast table when Emily went to light her cigarette.

A few hours and several cups of coffee later, she was still feeling that the world was not quite solid underfoot, that a heavy thump of her foot on the floor of the shop would shatter the brittle shell and send her hurtling into the dark.

The bell above the door tinkled periodically as people drifted in. Not that all of them were customers. Some were regulars, friends of Emily who dropped by for a chat. Others were browsers, who came in, took a turn or two around the shop, and left empty-handed.

Some people were drawn in by the display of books in the window, others by the books in the dollar bins outside, where Emily banished all books she didn't want. Some were students, some were businesspeople, some were residents of the neighborhood. Whoever they were, not enough of them were buying books.

In her brief time there, it had become clear to O that the shop was in dire trouble. It was a miracle Emily was able to make ends meet.

Some things were beyond their control. The neighborhood had changed. People's interests had changed. Not as many people were buying secondhand books. In fact, there were more people wanting to get rid of their book collections than there were people buying books. Hence the boxes of books Emily kept buying rather than see them thrown out.

There was nothing much that could be done about all that. But about other things, there was. Earlier that day, while O had been up the ladder shelving books, a young woman in her late twenties had wandered into the shop. Sunglasses perched on top of her head, expensive haircut, classy linen skirt, designer sandals. Obviously one of the café crowd, looking for a little something to read while sipping her latte on a patio in the sun.

The woman didn't venture far into the shop. Her invisible antennae had already alerted her to the fact that she was in alien territory. She gravitated to PAPERBACK LITERATURE – front room, rack nearest door, alphabetical by Author. It was like dipping your toe in the water at the beach without actually going in.

She scanned the outermost books on the rack, picked up one, and fanned through it. A puff of dust rose from the book, visible even to O atop the ladder. The woman ran her hand over the cover of the book, then looked at her fingers. She peered down into the dingy display window, up at O on her perch, then quietly returned the book to the rack and made her way out the door. The bell rang with an unmistakable finality behind her.

At that moment Emily, oblivious to the entire incident, called out to say there was another pile of books to shelve.

As O shelved the books, already moving with more confidence through the collection, she found herself feeling a strange mixture of emotions. She felt embarrassed by the condition of the shop, embarrassed that she had been dismissed in the same breath as it had been. At the same time, she felt angry – angry at the woman for being so shallow; angry at herself for being so vulnerable; angry at Emily for letting the shop slide so.

LITERARY CRITICISM – front room, left wall. She clambered up the ladder to the high shelves and squeezed one of the books Emily had handed her onto the already teeming shelf. From here, she had a bird's-eye view of the shop. Emily was sitting at her desk, smiling up at her in approval. O's anger melted and she managed a weak smile back.

For better or worse, the two of them were in this together. Emily hadn't let the shop slide because she'd wanted to. She was not well, though she did a good job of denying it. And she was getting older. Most people her age had already retired. But what was she to do? This shop was her life; she was in every dusty corner of it. Not only did she work here, she lived here. If the shop went under – and it seemed just a question of time before it did – what would she do? Where would she live?

O's vantage point from the top of the ladder suddenly gave her a new perspective on the problem. She was sure her father had no idea what he was sending her into. Emily was very good at candy-coating her situation. Her letters had not talked about the books that were accumulating at the bottom of the shelves for want of space. Her phone calls had not let out that little puff of dust that the book in PAPERBACK LITERATURE had let out. She was good at hiding the truth. She had always been a woman of secrets, and now the greatest secret was that under a veneer of stubborn independence stood someone in need of help.

Then and there, O decided she would do everything in her power to resurrect the Green Man. She couldn't do much about the changes in the book business, but she could do something about the dust and disorder that had settled over the shop.

She could clean the windows, vacuum the display area, lay new felt down in place of the dingy, sun-bleached stuff that was there now. She could paint the outside of the shop; maybe even give the Green Man sign a facelift. Just thinking of it all was exhausting. But she started down the ladder with a new sense of purpose.

—

It was then she noticed a tall lean boy, with deep hooded eyes and an unruly shock of dark hair, browsing through the bargain bins outside the shop. He was dressed all in black, with a knapsack draped over one shoulder. Something about him captivated her from the start. She couldn't keep her eyes off him.

O decided the feather duster needed shaking. She scrambled down the ladder and out the front door. The boy didn't bother to look up. She gave the duster a brisk shake. The dust plumed off it. He still didn't look up.

She thought about asking him if he needed any help, but by the time the thought made it from her mind to her mouth, he had wandered off down the street. She drifted back into the shop with the dust, wondering if this qualified as an encounter.

She spent the rest of the morning moving the dust around and rehearsing all the brilliant things she might have said.

13

O had been barely one month at the Green Man when, one morning over breakfast, Emily casually announced she had a doctor's appointment and wondered if O could open the shop and take care of things until she got back. She'd be just a couple of hours, she said. The thought of being left on her own at the shop for the first time filled O with panic, but in a moment of madness, she said she thought she could manage.

At ten o'clock sharp, with the cashbox tucked under her arm, O headed down to the shop. She switched on the lights, flipped the sign in the door window, and stepped outside. As she was cranking out the awning to give a bit of shade, she glanced up at the Green Man.

He looked back at her through his squinty eyes, and the vines spilled from his mouth in a silent greeting. At first she'd thought his forehead was furrowed in anger, but now she imagined it was only fatigue. He had seen many things over time. Since his face was carved on both sides of the sign, he looked forwards and backwards at once. He saw things coming, saw things going. He looked into the future, peered into the past – and swung back and forth like a doorway between them. She wished she could climb up closer to him. If she could just see him face-to-face, she felt some of the mystery surrounding him might fall away.

She dragged the bargain bins out and parked them in the shade under the window. As she tidied up the books a bit, her eyes kept drifting to the shop next door – Gigi's Patisserie. She had to force herself not to wander over and look in the window. Look in the window, and it was game over.

All it took was a little self-control. She headed straight back inside, fetched the duster from behind the desk, and walked briskly up and down the aisles, running it smartly along the edges of the lower shelves until they shone. The shop smelled of some sweet, gooey, chocolaty thing Gigi had been baking that morning.

She suddenly remembered that the bargain books had looked pretty dusty. It had been hot and dry for the past few days, and the dust from the street settled on them like crazy. She was certain no one wanted to look through bins of dusty books. She'd better give them a dusting, too, while she was at it. She headed back outside.

O was just going over them a second time when the door to the bakery opened and Gigi came out, carrying her signboard. Gigi was a perky young thing, with flaming red hair, piercings running up both ears, and a ruby stud in her nose. She had a sweet French accent that turned even a simple good morning into an event.

"Hey, O," she said.

They had met. Several times. A considerable portion of the Green Man's profits flew directly from the battered cashbox in the desk drawer into Gigi's till.

"Hi. What smells so good? I've been drooling all over the floor inside the shop."

Gigi laughed. "Chocolate éclairs," she said, pointing to the signboard where she'd written the daily specials in her curlicue writing. "Would you like to try one?"

"I shouldn't." Recently, she'd been trying to wean Emily off Gigi's decadent desserts in favor of carrot and celery sticks. She could use a little weaning herself.

"Don't be silly. It's on the house. It's the least I can do for smelling up your shop. Fred's just putting them out now."

Fred was a pastry chef who had been around the business for years. Gigi had hired him after a series of friends who'd come to work with her had all drifted off to less demanding work. Running a bakery was a killing business. Gigi and Fred were in the shop at five every morning, baking for the day ahead. Then, at the end of each day, they prepared the dough for the next day and let it rest overnight.

O followed Gigi into the bakery. Fred was arranging that day's baking in the window and gave her a friendly nod. Gigi had the most delicious window in Caledon. You could put on five pounds just looking in it.

Buttery madeleines, coconut-filled macaroons, crispy palmiers, gooey apple tarts, and tiny petits fours with pale pastel icing were ranged on the gleaming glass shelves. Inside were still more treasures: lemon tarts topped with chocolate strawberries and drizzled with apricot glaze; napoleons layered with rich pastry cream sandwiched between delicate sheets of golden puff pastry and sprinkled with icing sugar; melt-in-your-mouth butter cookies with bits of candied cherry on top; plump blueberry turnovers sprinkled with sugar; and decadent chocolate pies.

And, today, there was a tray of mouthwatering chocolate éclairs piped full of pastry cream and dipped in chocolate fondant. Gigi took one from the tray and put it on a napkin.

"Here you go. Let me know what you think."

"I think I've just died and gone to heaven."

Back inside the shop, O crawled into the bunker that was Emily's desk and switched on the radio. As she waited for the first customer to come through the door, she tallied the sales for the previous day and tidied the top of the desk as much as she dared. The chocolate éclair shrank down quickly to a sprinkling of crumbs on the crumpled napkin. She buried the evidence at the bottom of the wastebasket, where Emily would be unlikely to find it.

Feeling guilty, she grabbed the broom from the corner and did a quick sweep of the shop. Emily had been at the Green Man for so long that there were no longer any bare spaces on the walls. Pictures and posters and old flyers covered the ends of the bookcases and filled all the gaps between.

Most were pictures of poets – black-and-white plates that had come loose from old books, picture postcards, framed photos leaning on slack wires from the wall, looking down in quiet dismay at the clutter accumulating on the floor below. She recognized some, but many were simply nameless writers, dust settling on their unfathom-able faces. Emily talked about these dead poets as though they were still here, as if their pictures somehow sum-moned their presence.

O paused in the poetry section in front of a daguerre-otype of a young woman seated by a table with a book on it. One of the young woman's hands hung over the edge of the table and caught at a small posy of flowers in the other, in a silent, somehow desperate gesture. It was as if every part of her wanted to flee and she was held still by sheer force of will.

They had been introduced. Emily said this was the only known photo of the reclusive poet Emily Dickinson, who had spent the better part of her adult life hidden away from the world, refusing to venture beyond the high hedge that surrounded her parents' house and fleeing to the safety of her room when visitors came to call. O added her name to the list of mad poets.

The poet was dressed in a long-sleeved dark gown trimmed with lace at the neck. Her hair was parted in the center and drawn back over her ears. Her eyes were large and penetrating, and her lips were full. She seemed poised on the brink of speech.

The bell above the door jingled, jarring O back into reality. A young couple walked in carrying coffees. One of them was talking on a cell phone. O retreated behind the desk. They wandered around the front of the shop awhile, drifted into the back room, then finally came to the desk and asked if she had anything on computers.

They didn't know how funny that was. Obviously they hadn't seen the sun-bleached sticker on the front door – a picture of a computer surrounded by a red circle with a slash running through it. Emily was a bit of a fanatic when it came to computers. "Mark my words," she was fond of saying, "the computer and the book are not friends." Not only was there no computer, there was no television upstairs in the flat, either. Living at the Green Man was like taking a giant step back in time.

When she told the couple they had nothing on computers, they looked at one another in disbelief. As they made their way to the door, one of their phones rang and they both went for their pockets. The bell tinkled into silence behind them.

O busied herself with some books Emily had left for her to go through. One was on the figure of the Green Man. Emily had stuck a little note to it – *Thought you might be interested in this.*

She had just begun to flip through the book when she heard what sounded like a faint swish from somewhere inside the shop. Looking up, she wondered if someone could have stolen in without her noticing.

From the desk you could see only down the center aisle. The side aisles were obscured by the mountain of books on the desk, and the security mirrors mounted on the wall above them were too dimmed with dust to be of much use.

"Hello?" she called. There was no answer. She returned to the book. It was full of Green Men – carved on the tops of columns in old churches, hidden under the seats of choir pews, leaning out from the lintels above ancient doorways. Some of them looked much more frightening than their Green Man.

A few minutes later, O heard the swishing sound again. This time she got up from the desk, more curious than nervous. With the bakery right next door, mice were a fact of life in the Green Man, and Psycho was a touch too weird to be much of a mouser.

She stamped her foot to frighten any tiny intruder back into its hole and heard what sounded like a light patter of footsteps in response. She walked to the near end of the left-hand range. Peering down the aisle, she thought she caught a glimpse of something rounding the corner at the other end. It was just a glimpse, and the light diffused through the dusty window gave everything at the front of the shop a ghostly glow, but she could have sworn she'd seen a figure in a long gown.

"Is anyone there?" she called. Again, there was no reply. She walked to the front and stood at the door. The shop was empty, yet she felt sure someone had been there.

As she moved back through the shop, she paused in the poetry section to pick up a book lying open on the floor. Returning it to its place on the shelf, she noticed that several other books had been disturbed. The picture of the reclusive poet hung slightly askew on the wall. As she straightened it, O looked again into those wide knowing eyes. Working at the Green Man could definitely get to you. Just the other day, she'd briefly caught sight of the figure on the stairs. By the end of the summer, she was going to be as batty as Emily.

Back behind the desk, she plunged into the Green

Man book again. She learned that the Green Man had been adopted by medieval stonemasons and wood-carvers as their special symbol. They tucked the figure in out-of-the-way places in the vast cathedrals they built, as a sort of signature of their work. He was connected to what creativity meant for them. The vines that spilled from his mouth symbolized the outpouring of inspiration. He stood at the gateway between two worlds, at the place where imagination passed into creation.

14

The bell above the door tinkled lightly, and some-one entered the shop. A small man with wiry gray hair and a short sparse beard came walking down the aisle, carrying two large coffees. His forehead was furrowed; his bright blue eyes set in a permanent squint, as if he'd spent a lifetime working in the sun.

When he saw O sitting at the desk, he stopped short. Turning abruptly, he pretended to scan the shelves beside him as he worked his way slowly along the aisle and dis-appeared into the back room. O glanced up in the mirror mounted over the desk and saw him settle into the arm-chair. He set the two coffees down on the table.

He was definitely a little odd, and she kept looking up at the mirror to keep track of where he was. He had taken a large book from the art shelf and sat with it open on his lap, but whenever she looked up, she found him looking back, studying her suspiciously, as if he thought she might have kidnapped Emily and commandeered the shop.

A few minutes later, she glanced up from her work and found him standing by the desk, holding the two cups of coffee. She let out a little cry.

"Sorry to startle you," he said in a thin brittle voice. "I was wondering if Emily was around."

"She's gone to a doctor's appointment. She won't be back for an hour or so."

"I see. You know, you look remarkably like her. When I first saw you sitting there, I thought she'd found the fountain of youth."

O chuckled. "I'm her niece."

"Pleased to meet you. I'm Leonard Wellman. Your aunt and I are old friends."

"The poet Leonard Wellman?"

"Yes," he beamed. "Now how on earth would a young slip of a thing like you happen to know of an old fellow like me?"

"My father's a big fan of your work."

"Really. Well, I'm delighted to make your acquaintance –"

"O," she said. She noted how he took the name in stride.

"Well, O, would you like one of these coffees? I bought it for your aunt, actually. Double double, the way she likes it."

O took the coffee and sipped it while he continued to talk. It was lukewarm and very sweet. A few sips and she could feel the caffeine and sugar coursing through her veins.

Mr. Wellman – "Please, call me Leonard" – loosened up and was soon talking nonstop. It turned out Emily and he went way back. The way he spoke about her, O sensed that, at one time, they may have been more than friends.

"Here, let me show you something," he said. He put down his coffee and started along the left aisle toward the front of the shop. He paused in the literature section before a framed picture mounted below a photo of James Joyce. She had noticed the photo of Joyce before – his hair slicked back, his little mustache and thick round glasses – but she hadn't paid much attention to the picture beneath it.

It was a group shot – half a dozen people, three seated on a stuffed couch that looked somehow familiar, three others standing behind. She suddenly recognized the couch as the one in the back room, before Psycho had set her stamp on it. Then she noticed that the woman in the middle of the group on the couch was Emily – Emily about twenty-five years ago.

"Recognize anyone?" asked Leonard.

"Yes, that's my aunt," O said, pointing.

"And how about that good-looking guy standing right behind her?"

Although the figure in the photo had a thin mustache and a little goatee rather than the beard he had now, the wiry hair gave him away. "Is that you?"

"Indeed, it is. And that's James Woodruff, Letitia Boucher, Thomas Lodge, and Peter Camber – poets all. Three of them are dead. Letty's still with us – still writing, as far as I know. The photo was taken in the back room of the shop on the occasion of the first 'Tuesdays at the Green Man' gathering."

O gave him a puzzled look.

"Oh, so she hasn't told you about that."

She shook her head.

"Well, I can't see why she'd want to keep it a secret. Emily had just taken over the shop from the previous owner, who'd been a friend of mine. She told me she was thinking of starting up a reading group. She had the feeling there were other poets drifting around Caledon, looking for a home, and she wanted to provide that home – the opportunity for fellowship and sharing one's gifts.

"I jumped at the idea and offered to help her get it going. She decided the back room of the shop would be a perfect place to meet. We bought some secondhand folding chairs, put up flyers, placed an announcement in the local literary magazine, and waited to see what would happen.

"People began to come. A few at first, but more as word spread. We met the last Tuesday of the month. We called it Tuesdays at the Green Man. There would usually be one or two guest readers, then for the second half, we'd throw the floor open to whoever wanted to read from their work. On a good night, we might have two dozen people in that room.

"I used to look forward to that meeting all month – and I'm sure I wasn't the only one. It was a chance to come together with other poets, to meet old friends, and to make new ones, all in an atmosphere of books. Several important poets had their start here. We'd set up a 'sale table,' where the guest readers on any given night could sell their books. And Emily would always be sure to buy a couple of copies to put on the shelves.

"This became a place for poets to escape the terror of the empty page, to find inspiration, to take delight in the companionship of others in the same boat. And it was a rare chance to read new work to an appreciative and responsive audience.

"I'm making it sound like a paradise, I know. And it certainly wasn't that. We had our petty grievances, our little spats. But all of us knew we had found a very good thing. And it was your aunt who quietly held it together – not so much by what she said as by her mere presence. Poets are creatures attuned to silence, and Emily was the queen of silence. But, oh, such speaking silence. You can feel it in every line she wrote.

"She gave her quiet encouragement to all who met here.

She had her depths – which we dared not plumb – her secrets, her solitude; but so had we, every one. She understood that, and she allowed us the space to grow. That was her great virtue. It was what drew those who had stumbled on the meeting by chance to return by choice.

"We had our share of eccentrics, those whose lives ran in less than regular channels. But everyone was welcome, and somehow we all got along. We made friends we cared for and who cared for us. They were good times. We even took a stab at starting up a small press to publish poetry."

O was fascinated by Leonard's story. She had no idea her aunt had been involved in such a thing. "What happened to the readings?" she wondered aloud as they wandered back to the desk. "Why did they stop?"

"Well, actually," said Leonard, "they were still going until quite recently. Not nearly as vital as they had been at the beginning, mind you. But, then again, neither are we. Money became a problem. As our original members grew older and our numbers dwindled, we needed to bring in new blood. But that demanded outreach, which in turn demanded money. And there was precious little of that as times changed and the business began to suffer. Emily was no longer able to just dip into the till to pay the guest readers and to help fund the refreshments. Between one thing and another, our little group was languishing, and it seemed only a matter of time before the readings would become a thing of the past.

"And then your aunt had her attack. It was serious – though she prefers to gloss over it. I know, because I'm the one who found her."

"Really?"

"Yes. I was dropping by for my regular visit. I live out of town now, but I manage to make it in about once a month. I had some news that day. I'd heard through the grapevine that the Caledon Arts Council had some new money available for arts groups, and I thought, why not our little group? So I went to speak to someone on the council, got all the information, and made the grant application.

"I came into the shop, feeling very optimistic about the future and dying to share the news with Emily. I found her sitting right where you are now. I knew straightaway there was something seriously wrong. Her color was off, and she sat dead still, as if she'd turned to stone. It was all she could do to whisper."

"What did she say?"

"She said she felt very peculiar. There was a pain like a vice around her chest. Well, it didn't take much to know she was having a heart attack. She didn't want to go to hospital – she has always had a terror of doctors – but I insisted, and she was in no shape to object.

"I took her down in my car. She refused to go in an ambulance, said she didn't want the neighbors to see that. The doctors confirmed it had been a heart attack. These things often come in pairs, so they insisted on keeping her in hospital overnight for observation. They told her she'd have to be very careful. The next one could well be more serious, perhaps even fatal."

O was hearing more about her aunt's condition than Emily had ever told her.

"She seemed a little subdued after that," Leonard went on. "Preoccupied, I guess you'd say. I'm sure it must have frightened her, made her see that she was on closer terms with Death than she'd imagined. But I sensed there was something else." He shook his head.

"As time passed, she became more her old self – smoking too much, not eating properly, not taking her pills. She continued to put in her time here too, of course. The shop stayed open as it always had, but some things she'd been able to do before seemed suddenly beyond her. I guess that's one of the reasons why you're here. She told me you were coming. She thinks very highly of you and your father."

"Yeah, that's why I'm here, I guess. Though I think my aunt would like to believe she's the one taking care of me."

"That sounds like Emily, all right," he said with a laugh. "You know, I think I can already see signs of your handiwork around here. The place is looking much better than the last time I was in."

O beamed. At that moment, the door opened and the mailman came in. He was wearing shorts and a sun hat and had a can of mace clipped to his mailbag. He handed O a bundle of mail banded together with an elastic, wished them both a good day, and left.

"So there haven't been any readings since Emily's attack?" asked O.

"No, she hasn't so much as mentioned it, to tell the truth. I'm not even sure she's writing right now."

"And what about the grant?"

"I haven't heard anything yet, I'm afraid."

He downed the last of his coffee and dropped the paper cup in the wastebasket beside the desk. "Well, I suppose I should be going. It was a pleasure meeting you, O. I'm sure we'll see one another again."

"Yes, I hope so," said O.

After Leonard was gone, she wandered into the back room. Things that had been a mystery to her before were suddenly made clear. Like the folding chairs stacked against the wall, the small raised platform at the far end of the room – and the reference to this as the Gathering Room in the Subject Guide to the Green Man, when the only things that seemed to gather here were empty boxes and dust.

Standing in the doorway, O imagined what it might be like with the chairs set out and a crowd of people quietly listening as someone filled the room with the sound of poetry.

15

"Leonard Wellman dropped by while you were out."

"Really. How did he seem?"

"Very well. He sends you his best."

"He's a dear soul. And a darned good poet."

They were cleaning up after dinner. While Emily stacked the dirty dishes on the counter, O ran water in the sink. The kettle rattled on the burner as it came to a boil.

"Did he stay long?"

"Not too long. It took him awhile to work up the nerve to talk to me. He said he thought at first I was you – that you'd discovered the fountain of youth."

"That's very funny."

As Emily set the dishes down on the counter beside her, O caught the faint odor of cigarette smoke. So perhaps she hadn't quit completely, after all. O wondered how many other things were being hidden from her. She shut off the water and started washing the dishes, putting them on the draining board to drip.

"How was the doctor's appointment?"

"You know, there's something about sitting in a waiting room full of heart patients. You can almost hear their minds whirring, wondering which of them will croak first."

"That's just your imagination."

"Exactly." She picked up a tea towel and began to dry.

"What did the doctor say?"

"My cholesterol levels are a little better – probably thanks to you. He's still not happy about the blood pressure, though. He wants me to try another pill. I'm going to have to build an addition onto the medicine chest! Oh, and he said I should get more exercise. I'm too sedentary, he says. Good Lord, I'm seventy years old."

O could imagine how difficult it would be to have Emily as a patient. She was cantankerous at the best of times, and she didn't take well to being told what to do. The kettle came to the boil. Emily dropped two bags into the teapot and poured the steaming water over them.

O took a deep breath. "Leonard was telling me about the poetry readings you used to have here."

Silence.

"He showed me the photo of you and him and the other early members."

More silence, broken only by the sound of the lid of the teapot being put in place, the clatter of cups and saucers being set out – one set deliberately mismatched.

"And what else did he tell you?"

"Just what a wonderful thing the readings were. How important you had been to a lot of young poets."

"Leonard talks too much." She began hunting through the cupboards. "What happened to those cookies I bought?"

"You ate them."

"All of them?"

"Yup."

"That can't be true. You must have had some."

"Not one. They had coconut in them. I'm allergic. I eat coconut, my throat closes, I die."

"Really?"

"Uh-huh."

Emily stirred the tea in the pot with a spoon – just in case it wasn't strong enough already – and poured it into the cups. She took the mismatched cup and saucer for herself and gave the other to O. What she really wanted, O suspected, was to light up a cigarette. Cigarettes calmed her, and talking about the readings had obviously touched a nerve.

"Why do you always do that?" asked O.

"What?"

"Mismatch your cup and saucer like that?"

"Just to be perverse, I suppose." She fiddled with the handle of her cup, scratched her neck, and ran her fingertips over the skin. It was red and angry looking. Likely a reaction to all the chocolate she'd been eating since trying to cut out the cigarettes. But this wouldn't be a good time to bring that up.

Emily sat staring at her cup. She had dropped down into one of the mind chasms she regularly fell into. After a couple of minutes, she clambered back out.

"When I was young, there were coffeehouses where poetry readings regularly took place. There were small magazines, where new work was published, small presses devoted to publishing poetry. None of them made any money, of course, but that wasn't the point. I don't think any of us ever expected to make a living at it. We were happy just practicing the craft, carrying on an honorable tradition."

While she talked, she turned the cup around on the saucer.

"It was exotic to be a poet in those days. There was excitement in the air. People were bursting with ideas, eager to break new ground. It's not like that now. Poets are an endangered species. They don't appear on the WWF list, but they're every bit as endangered. I don't know how anyone even begins to write poetry these days, or how they keep at it. It's a lonely business – you don't write poetry in an office pool; you write it alone. But where are the supports now? Where is the audience? They simply don't exist."

O had heard enough. "Maybe that's why the Green Man readings were so important," she said. Emily looked up at her. O swallowed hard and went on.

"I mean, if it's true that poets are more isolated than ever, aren't they even more in need of supports like that? And if the people who provide them grow discouraged and give up, don't they just become part of the problem?"

She'd said more than she meant to, and far more bluntly than she should have. You could have cut the silence with a knife.

Emily rose from the table and took her cup to the counter. Disappearing down the hall, she came back moments later with her sweater and her purse. "I'm going for a walk," she said. "I shouldn't be long."

Translation: *I'm totally ticked off with you, and I'm going out for a cigarette.*

O sat at the table for a while, rehearsing her apology for being impertinent as her tea grew cold. An hour later, her aunt still hadn't returned.

As she waited, O slipped off the elastic from the bundle of mail that had been delivered to the shop that morning and went through it. Junk mail and bills. Then, at the bottom of the pile, a letter addressed to her. It was from her father. She retreated to her room, where she could read it undisturbed.

He thanked her for her letter and was glad to hear she was doing well and adapting to living with Emily. He reminded her that Emily might be a little crusty on the outside, but that she had a heart of gold underneath it all.

O read happily along, hearing the sound of his voice in the words and missing him. In her letter to him, she'd mentioned that, though he was in Italy, Emily had recently seen him staring in the shop window one afternoon, looking not as he did now but as he'd looked as a boy. She also mentioned seeing the same boy on the wall.

When she wrote the letter, she'd wondered whether she should mention it at all. She didn't want him thinking they were both losing their minds. So she'd just tossed off a couple of sentences at the end, making light of the whole affair. His response surprised her.

On your last birthday I gave you a little silver pendant in the shape of a hand. I told you that someone had given it to me a long time ago, when I was about your age. That someone was a mysterious girl I happened to meet one summer day. She'd somehow lost her memory, and I walked with her through Caledon, hoping something we saw might jog it back.

It was a hot day, and at one point we stopped under the awning of a bookshop to get some shade. That shop was the Green Man. As I was looking in the window, I noticed someone at the back of the shop – an older woman, smoking a cigarette and carrying an armload of books. She glanced toward the front and saw me there.

The woman I saw was Emily – not as she was then, a young woman in her twenties, but as she is now. I think she must have recognized me, because she walked toward me. But just then I realized the girl I was with had wandered off. There was no telling where she might go, so I hurried after her.

I found her at the end of the dead-end street that ran beside the shop. She climbed on top of the wall there and went over. So I followed her. But as I was sitting on the wall, I took one last look back toward the shop. All I could see from there was the back of the building. A door opened on the top floor and a girl came out onto the deck, carrying a box. She looked down and saw me, and a strange expression came over her face. I didn't know why then, but I do now. That girl was you, looking back through some seam in time at the boy who would one day become her father.

The girl I was walking with finally did remember who she was. When we said good-bye, she gave me the pendant that I gave to you.

All these things that I was sure were lost down a tunnel of time forever have suddenly come back. My grandmother once told me that nothing ever vanishes. Everything is always here, is always now. I didn't know what she meant then, but I think I do now. I told you the Green Man was a remarkable place. Take care of yourself, O, and take care of Emily. Write again soon.

Lots of love,
Dad

She folded the letter and tucked it away in her journal. The room had begun to fill with shadows. A sense of strangeness lay over everything. She had the sudden awareness of things existing not only in space, but also in time. From the pictures on the wall to the paperweights on the dresser, from the books on the shelves to the curtains in the window – everything was steeped in time. The door that separated past from present had, for some reason, opened here. She wondered what else might slip through.

The spell was broken by the sound of Emily returning from her walk. She called up the stairs to say that she'd picked up a tub of ice cream from one of the shops down the street and it was melting fast.

O realized this was Emily's way of saying she was sorry for the wedge that had come between them. She hurried downstairs, and soon they were sitting together at the table, basking in the bliss of Chocolate Delight.

16

The call that was to change everything came a week later, while O was on duty at the shop. It was Saturday, and Emily had gone off in the car to do a sweep of the local yard sales, searching for treasures. The panic O had first felt at being left alone in the shop had diminished to a vague unease.

Good-weather days were as bad for the book business as bad-weather days. And today the weather was sunny and warm. Across the street, Tiny, the owner of the Mind Spider Tattoo Parlor, was sitting shirtless outside his shop, catching some rays while he read the latest Gothic romance he'd picked up at the Green Man.

Tiny was a pretty scary-looking guy, as were many of those who frequented his shop. He looked as if he might have been a biker in a former life; but, in this one, he was a total pussycat. He and Gigi had taken Emily under their wing and watched out for her. They both dropped by the shop on a pretty regular basis.

Tiny made quite a sight. His upper body was completely covered in tattoos. He was a big man, so he was wearing a lot of ink. Between that and the piercings, he attracted a fair bit of attention from passersby. He waved in greeting as O dragged out the bargain bins and rolled down the awning.

The bookshop was definitely in better shape than it had been when she first came. She'd spent the last several days clambering up and down the ladder, hauling armloads of books for Emily to weed through, giving the shelves a good cleaning while they were empty, then putting the books that had passed inspection back into place.

The rejects were consigned to empty boxes – some for the bargain bins, some for the rehab hospital, the rest for Goodwill.

It was hard for Emily to part with her stock, even things she knew had sat untouched on the shelves for years. But, as the days went by, she began to relax her standards a little. So far they had filled close to two dozen boxes. Suddenly there was space on the shelves for the books that had been multiplying on the floor.

Much was still to be done, but today it was simply too hot to bother. The shop was like an oven. The least exertion caused streams of sweat to start pouring down O's face. She sat at the cluttered desk, cleaning and pricing a stack of paperbacks Emily had left for her, sipping on a can of iced tea. It had been refreshingly cold when she first opened it an hour ago, but now it was warm and sweet, with a disturbingly chemical aftertaste. The fan, ancient and definitely lacking the Safety Association stamp of approval, sat on the windowsill beside her and blew the warm air halfheartedly around. Even the music drifting from the radio seemed weary with the heat.

She sprayed a little Windex on a cloth and wiped down the covers. Then she fanned through the books to check for markings and for anything that had been left behind. After erasing a few light pencil markings, she wrote the selling price on the first page. Generally, they charged half the initial price of the book. She set the books aside for Emily to check later, before they were put up on the shelves.

The night before, O had started working on a poem. A few random lines came to her as she lay down to sleep. Words often decided to come then. She tumbled out of bed, sat at the desk, and wrote them down. She crossed some words out, tried others and crossed them out as well. A pool of light shone on the page. She felt the silence pressing in like darkness all around. She pierced it with the pen, and words trickled out.

Now she took the folded piece of paper from her pocket and looked at the poem in the clear light of day. She called it "Garden Sculpture."

Winter has not been kind to you.
Frost has crept into the crevices
Of your features,
Worn the fine details dull.
From a distance you are snow,
Impossible survivor of the lost
Kingdom of zero.

She changed a word here, added another there. With a little fiddling, she was able to find a way past the impasse she had reached the night before.

You bear disfigurement
Without complaint,
Look skyward with blue amaze,
Oblivious of blinding sun,
Like one long shut in prison
Dreams of day – then wakes
To find it come.

Something in the musty, dusty perfume of the Green Man inspired poetry. Perhaps it was because this was a place where poetry had happened, and happened over a good many years. It was a place the muse knew and visited with some regularity – even if no one else did.

—

The phone rang. It was an old phone. Emily preferred her machines old. New things made her nervous. As if to compensate for its age, the phone had a very virile ring. It had just launched into a second one, when O plucked up the receiver and stopped it short.

"Hello. Green Man bookshop."

"Hello. May I speak to Emily Endicott, please?" It was an older woman's voice. Very proper, with the whisper of an accent O couldn't place.

"I'm sorry, she's not in at the moment. May I take a message?" She grabbed a scrap of paper and a pencil.

"Yes. This is Lenora Linton speaking. Miss Endicott doesn't know me, but I should like to speak to her about a personal library I would like to sell."

"I see." Just what they needed – more books.

"I'll leave my number with you. She can call and arrange a time to see the collection, if she's interested." She gave a local number.

"There's just one more thing. Time is of the essence in this matter. The collection must be sold within a month."

"I understand," said O. She glanced up to check the calendar for when that would be. There was a bare space on the wall where the calendar should have been. Emily must have taken it down for some reason. She wrote *Must be sold in a month's time* on the piece of paper, along with the rest of the information.

"Very well, then. I look forward to hearing from Miss Endicott at her earliest convenience. Good-bye."

"Good-bye," said O, but the phone had already gone dead.

She put down the receiver and stuck the message to the arm of the lamp, where Emily would be sure to see it.

She had just turned back into her poem, when the bell above the door chimed. She glanced up to see who the first customer of the day might be. Her heart gave a little flutter. It was him – the boy she'd seen browsing through the bargain bins last week. Now here he was inside the shop, and she was alone with him. She thought she might faint.

He was younger than he'd seemed the first time she saw him. She realized with a shock that he couldn't be much older than her – sixteen, seventeen at most. He was very good looking, but not in your typical buff, blue-eyed, chisel-chinned, fashion-model sort of way. No, he was more exotic than that, with a smoldering edge to him.

He wore black pants and a black jacket over a white tee shirt. His backpack hung from one shoulder. He had a cool rumpled look about him, his hair all this way and that, like he'd just tumbled out of bed.

His features were finely tooled, his mouth full and red against the almost marble pallor of his face. He was almost *too* good looking. As he ventured farther into the shop, he glanced her way. She caught a glimpse of those dark dangerous eyes and realized at once she was in the presence of mystery.

Her heart raced. Part of it was the nervousness she felt whenever she was alone in the shop, but more of it was because she was alone with *him*. She tried to calm herself, breathing steadily, evenly. She didn't dare look his way. Instead, she pretended to be busy. She fussed about the desk, wrapped the dust jackets of a couple of hardcover books in plastic, walked a couple of paperbacks she'd just finished pricing to the racks at the front of the shop. In fact, though, she was busy only with him.

The boy took no notice of her. Despite that, perhaps because of it, he compelled her attention. She watched closely as he climbed the ladder and stretched to see the stock on the highest shelves, quietly moving with the poise and assurance of someone much older. She couldn't explain it, but the air in the shop was charged with a palpable tension that set her all on edge. He drew her, yet frightened her at the same time.

He settled finally in the poetry section. This immediately piqued her interest, for here was the beating heart of the Green Man. Emily kept the poetry section where she could keep an eye on it. So as the boy browsed through the several shelves that made up the collection, O was able to observe him through a gap between two piles of books on the desk. She watched him take down the volume of Keats, the little paperback of Milton in the mottled cover, the Rilke odes, Rexroth's translations of Chinese poems – all things she herself had looked through.

She watched him leaf through them, pause here and there to read a few lines, then return them to their place on the shelf. He handled books with the care of someone who loved them.

You could tell a good deal about a person from their hands. And this boy had the lean veined hands of an artist. They were pure poetry to watch. She wondered where he had come from, how he happened to stumble on the Green Man. He didn't strike her as a local, but an outsider, like herself.

While she sat watching him, she spun a story about him. He had lived in the country, a lonely child suffocated by the affections of a doting mother. But he was an artist, and when he couldn't take it anymore, he'd fled. For whatever reason, his travels had taken him to Caledon. She imagined he had only recently arrived. There was still a fluttery look about him, as though he had not yet settled his feathers.

She wondered how she would react if he came to the desk to buy a book. She wished the desk were not so cluttered, so chaotic, but at this point housekeeping was not an option. She looked down at the little poem she'd been working on when he came into the shop. Afraid he might catch sight of it if he headed her way, she quietly tucked it under a book and busied herself with clearing a little space in the clutter.

The boy stood in the poetry section for a long time. He had stopped going through the books and was just standing there. She sensed something was wrong. She was summoning her courage to wander over and ask him if he needed help finding anything, when suddenly, in one quick fluid motion, he plucked a book from the shelf, flicked open his jacket, and slipped it inside. Bending down, he picked up his backpack and sauntered out of the shop.

O watched in stunned disbelief. Emily had warned her to keep her eyes open for book thieves. With the desk positioned as it was, at the back of the shop, there was ample opportunity and easy escape for anyone who might want to pocket a book.

She told herself she must have been mistaken. She got up and walked over to the poetry section, her legs wobbling, her heart beating like a bird's. There was a gap in the middle of the *P* section. Emily was bound to notice. The woman had some kind of weird radar when it came to such things. O shifted a few books over to close the gap on the shelf, then went out the front door of the shop and looked up and down the street. There was no sign of the boy.

For the rest of the day, she could think of nothing but him.

17

"Lenora Linton? *The* Lenora Linton? I thought she was dead."

"Well, that would explain the bad connection." Emily gave her a look.

"Who *is* Lenora Linton, anyway?" O was up on the ladder, shelving the batch of books she had priced that morning, now that Emily had given them her stamp of approval.

"Lenora Linton is the great-granddaughter of Lawrence Linton."

"And who was he?"

"Lawrence Linton was one of the most important architects in Caledon's history. There are examples of his work everywhere: the old city hall, St. Bartholomew's Church, many of the buildings at the university, in addition to a good number of the grand old houses around town. The old Caledon train depot was his as well, come to think of it."

"Not the depot I saw."

"No, there was another depot before that, in a different part of town. It burned to the ground." She dropped down one of those mind chasms for a moment and was somewhere far away.

"It was Lawrence Linton who brought the Gothic Revival to Caledon," she continued. "Caledon was a little backwater town when he arrived. But soon towers and turrets and pointed arches were everywhere. Over time, tastes changed. Gothic architecture fell out of favor, and Linton's work was eclipsed by newer, more modern styles. He came to a curious end, as I recall."

"Curious? How do you mean?"

"Something happened to him. He spent his last years living alone in the big old house he'd built as a monument to the Gothic style."

"What was it that happened?"

"I'm not sure. There may be something about him in the local history section in the back room, if you're interested. In any event, I'd better call Lenora Linton and see what she has to say."

While Emily made the call, O finished shelving the books. She thought about what Emily had said about Lawrence Linton and wondered what had happened to turn him into a recluse. But apart from a couple of references to his buildings and a grainy photograph of Linton in middle age, there was nothing in LOCAL HISTORY to shed any light on it.

Emily was clearly excited when she hung up the phone. "It *was the* Lenora Linton – still very much among the living. She was very complimentary. Said I came highly recommended to her. By whom? I wonder. All very curious, but flattering nonetheless. At any rate, I'm to get first look at the collection. It could be a gold mine.

"She wants me to come around tomorrow afternoon. She still lives in the old family house. Just to see the inside of that place will be well worth the visit. Perhaps you'd like to come along. I could probably use your help."

For the rest of the day, Emily walked around on cloud nine. And it wasn't just the prospect of seeing inside the Linton house that made her that way; it was the dream of hitting the mother lode – something all book dealers dreamt of. It would be the answer to all their troubles. It would take the business from the edge of the cliff, where it teetered now, and set it back on solid ground.

That evening, while O was up in her room reading *A Treasury of Great Poems* and doing her best not to think of her book thief, she stumbled on another mad poet.

John Clare was born in England in 1793 to a poor farming family. One day, when he was five years old, he set out across the fields for the horizon, where he imagined the end of the world lay. There he hoped to look down from the edge and see into all the secrets of the world. He walked all day, but never seemed to come any closer, so he turned back. When he finally made his way home late that night, he found half the village out searching for him and his parents at their wits' end.

Though he had little formal education, in his late teens he began to write poetry. His first collection was a great success, and the "peasant poet" was the toast of London society for a short time. Within a few years, however, he was all but forgotten.

He had married at the height of his fame. Now, with a large family to support and no money coming in, he went back to working the fields. He hawked his books from door to door, often dragging a large sack of them thirty miles a day.

The strain of it proved too much. By the time he was forty, he began to experience fits of madness. He imagined he was married to a girl he had known as a boy and had several children by her. He saw visionary creatures and had conversations with Shakespeare's spirit. He was finally admitted to an asylum as one "addicted to writing poetry." He spent the last twenty-three years of his life there and continued writing to the end.

O had just closed the book on John Clare, when Emily called up the stairs, asking if she could come down for a minute. She felt sure her aunt had noticed the missing book in the poetry section and was going to ask who had bought it.

She found Emily at the kitchen table, sipping a cup of tea. Psycho was sitting on her lap. The cat took one look at O and sped off down the hall.

"Would you like some tea, O?"

"Sure. I'll get a cup." As she sat down at the table, she tried to read her aunt's face. The tea was so strong that you could have stood a spoon in it. She reached for the milk.

Then she saw the poem – *her* poem – there on the table in front of Emily. She realized she'd accidentally left it on the desk downstairs, and a sinking feeling hit her in the pit of her stomach.

"I take it this is yours," said Emily, picking up the sheet.

O nodded. If she had been a crazy white cat, she would have disappeared down the hall.

"Do you have more?" asked Emily.

"Yes."

"May I see them?"

"They're not very good."

"Don't worry. They never are. You write one so the next will come. And you hope, when it does, it will be a little better than the last."

"I'll be right back." O ran up to her room and returned

with her folder of poems. She flipped through them and found a recent piece.

"I'm a little afraid," she confessed.

"Me, too – all the time. There's a lot to be afraid of."

O took a deep breath, fought back the panic, and read the poem:

> *"Poems must be more*
> *Than just words dancing*
> *On the marble floor of the page*
> *To soft music*
> *In worn satin shoes.*
> *This bakery window,*
> *Its treasures tiered*
> *On stanzas of glass,*
> *Is a poem too . . ."*

As she read, her voice stopped quavering and she grew more at ease. When she finished, she looked over at Emily.

"I see now why you were so vocal about the Tuesdays," said her aunt. "It seems your father was right."

"About what?"

"About you. He said you might have the makings of a poet."

But there was something odd in the way she said it, something unsettling in the look on her face as she stared down at her tea. Finally, she leaned forward across the table.

"I need to warn you," she whispered, as though someone might be listening. "Poetry is nothing to be dabbled in. It can be a dangerous thing. Before you go one step farther, I want you to ask yourself if you absolutely have to do it, if something inside you will die if you don't. If the answer is no, then let it go."

O wasn't sure what reaction she'd been expecting from her aunt. Perhaps a little encouragement or support. Certainly not this. She felt angry and hurt. If she stayed one minute longer, she would start to cry – and that was the last thing in the world she wanted Emily to see.

Without a word, O scooped up her poems and ran upstairs to her room, closing the door behind her. She flung the folder down on the desk and threw herself on the bed. Why would Emily talk to her like that? Why would she try to warn her away from writing poetry, as if it were some private club only the truly mad could join? How could it be as dangerous as she made it seem?

The room was suddenly too small to hold her. Her thoughts bounced off the low ceiling, banging against the windowpane like a trapped bird. She needed air and space. Grabbing her notebook and pen from the desk, she crawled out through the window onto the deck and plopped herself down in the plastic chair. She took a deep breath and tried to blow her anger away.

The sun was low and the wind was up, whipping the treetops like a boy beating the bushes with a stick. Up here, with the wide sky spread before her and the dying light weaving its spell, her anger slowly ebbed away, and a calm came over her.

Into that calm came a word, then a line. She reached for her book and wrote it down. Another came, and then another in its wake. She had no idea where they came from, where they led. She listened, she wrote. It was as simple as that. She kept her head down like a swimmer in deep water, reaching out stroke after stroke, buoyed up by blind faith alone.

When inspiration passed, she had two pages of close scrawl. She looked down at the dim sheets. Never before had words flowed out of her like that.

When she first crawled out onto the rooftop deck, O had felt shut up in herself, trapped in a dark well whose high sides she could not hope to scale. But now she was free. She was the wide sky scattered with stars, the wind tossing among the trees.

Slowly she became herself again. She looked out the windows that were her eyes and said, *I am here.*

It was then she heard the noise – a light rattling that seemed to be coming from behind the building. She wondered if it had been going on all the time she was writing.

There it was again. She'd heard odd noises before, when she was sitting on the deck at night. The bakery next door put its garbage cans out back, behind the building, and Emily was constantly complaining about the vermin they attracted.

But this didn't sound like the scrabbling of rats. Perhaps a dog was nosing around the bins. She tried to catch her last thought before it drifted away. But she was too late – it was gone. The noise kept on.

Now her curiosity was up. She quietly closed her note-book and put it on the table. Then she heard something that sounded remarkably like a cough. That was definitely no dog down there, but a larger creature of the two-legged variety. She eased herself from her chair and crept toward the edge of the deck.

With each step, her feet crunched down in the loose gravel. She paused to see if she had alerted the intruder to her presence. But the quiet rattling continued.

As she neared the edge of the deck, she went down on her hands and knees and crawled the last couple of feet, until she came to the low brick wall that enclosed the deck. Taking a deep breath, she leaned just far enough over the edge to see down below.

The noise was definitely coming from behind the bakery. Someone was down there, rooting among the half a dozen large aluminum garbage cans ranged along the wall. The scavenger was working the lid off the last of them now. His back was to her, and she could make out nothing but the top of his head.

He got the lid off and set it quietly on the ground. The can was full of buns and bread. He stuffed as much as he could into his sack. The bakery was famous in the neighborhood, not only for its fancy French pastries, but for its bread and buns. At the end of the day, all the unsold baking was bagged as day-olds. But on Saturdays, whatever was left had to be thrown out. It went directly from the gleaming glass display windows out front to the battered containers out back.

The scavenger seemed to know the schedule. It was Saturday night, and here he was. There was something familiar about him, but the thought had only half-formed in O's mind when it was suddenly shattered by a noise behind her. She turned her head and saw Emily standing framed in the window of the attic room.

"What on earth are you doing out there?" said her aunt.

Her voice was loud enough to startle the scavenger at his work. He swung his head up in the direction of the deck. O jerked back quickly from the edge, hoping she hadn't been seen. A clatter resounded below, followed by hurried footsteps.

She looked down in time to see a dark figure with a backpack slung over one shoulder disappear down the lane.

18

Sunday the shop was closed. They slept in late, ate a hurried lunch, then headed for the car. It wouldn't start. Emily got out and kicked it. It still didn't start, but it seemed to make her feel better.

"What do we do now?" asked O.

"Walk, I guess. It's not that far."

In a bid to economize, O had suggested they bring coffees from home. The idea was that they would drink them comfortably in the car and leave the cups there. Now they sipped while they walked, sloshing coffee all over the street and looking like a couple of total losers.

Emily's sense of distance left something to be desired. They walked for what felt like an hour. The neighborhoods grew increasingly upscale – wide, deep lots; large old houses set far back from the street; immaculate lawns; cars that would always start on the first try, parked two abreast in the driveways.

O was almost glad Emily's car hadn't started. It would have looked painfully out of place alongside the Porches and BMWs that hung out here. It was easier to tuck a coffee cup out of sight than a car. She dumped the dregs onto the road and walked with her cup down at her side.

The streets looped and twisted like Psycho's knotted ball of wool. Emily had a puzzled look on her face, as if she wasn't quite sure where they were.

As they walked along, a man in a silk dressing gown opened his front door and plucked his paper from where it was wedged in the porch railing. He gave them a look that said *you definitely are not from around here*, and then retreated back into his house.

"Could you please finish that coffee?" said O. "It must be stone-cold by now, and we look like a pair of freaks carrying these old cups."

"You worry too much about what people think. If you really want to be a poet, the first requirement is a tough skin."

O realized this was as close to an apology for last night as she was likely to get. They walked along quietly for a while.

"I've been thinking about the Tuesdays," said Emily. O's ears perked up. "Do you know why we decided on Tuesday as the day?"

O shook her head.

"It was all because of Mallarmé."

Mallarmé was the ghost who sat midway on the stairs

between the shop and the flat, the one they both side-stepped now on their way up and down.

"Mallarmé was a French poet who lived at the end of the nineteenth century," continued Emily. "He believed that the power of poetry lay in its suggestiveness, that the aim of poetry was to evoke the mystery at the heart of things. In his work, he aimed to depict not the object, but the effect it produced.

"He worked slowly and published little. People found his work difficult, and he was attacked by the critics for his obscurity. He supported his family by working as an English teacher. He wasn't much of a teacher, but he was a great poet.

"Gradually, he attracted a following among the younger poets of the day. A group of them began meeting at Mallarmé's house on Tuesday evenings to read and discuss poetry. In French, Tuesday is *mardi*. These meetings became known as the *Mardis*, and those who attended them, the *Mardistes*. So when we decided to start up a poetry-reading group, I thought about Mallarmé. I suggested we meet one Tuesday a month and call it Tuesdays at the Green Man.

"I've been thinking about what you said. You were right; the meetings were a good thing. I've been distracted lately, and I've let things slide. If you're willing to lend a hand, I'd like to get the Tuesdays up and running again."

"Great!"

"But promise me you won't expect too much of them. These are not Mallarmé's *Mardis*."

"I promise." The street they were walking along now looked disturbingly familiar. "I think we're going in circles," she said.

Emily looked back uncertainly over her shoulder.

"You have no idea where we are, do you?" said O.

"Nonsense," said Emily. She had worn a tweed skirt and matching jacket for the occasion, but had long since shed the jacket in the heat. She walked with it hooked it over her arm.

O had worn her Sunday best as well, including a new pair of leather flats, little suspecting they would have to hike for over an hour to get to the house. The shoes pinched her toes and had rubbed her heel raw.

None of it did the least bit of good, anyway. They still looked like a pair of interlopers from the lower world. Finally, as they rounded yet another corner, O glanced up and saw the name of the street they'd been searching for. It was a short dead-end street. At the far end, a large old house sat peering over the top of a high hedge at them.

"There it is," said Emily exultantly. "I told you I wasn't lost."

—

There were only two other houses on the street, one on either side of the narrow road leading up to the Linton house. Both appeared deserted – their lawns gone wild, their windows boarded over. As they started down the street, O saw a large wrecking machine nestled in the shade at the side of one of the houses. It had fed on the side wall of the house, exposing the interior. She caught a glimpse of flowered wallpaper, a ceiling fixture dangling from a wire. She felt as if she'd come upon some fantastic beast in the midst of consuming its prey.

So far the Linton house had been spared the fate of its neighbors, but it hunched down behind the hedge and gave them a wary look through its windows as they turned up the walk.

In its day, the house would have been a Gothic dream, with its fanciful turret, high-pitched roof, pointed arches, and elaborately carved stonework. But time had taken its toll. The figures tooled in the soft limestone had weath-ered, and much of the detail had worn away, so that they seemed now like strange creatures in the midst of forming. Thick branches of ivy gripped the walls in a grim embrace.

"We can't go in there with these," said O, holding up her coffee cup. Rosebushes flanked the walk on either side. She took a quick look around, then reached in and wedged her cup in the crook of a branch. Emily followed suit, but thorns raked the back of her hand as she pulled it out.

"Ow!" she cried, clutching it with her other hand.

As they started up the steps of the covered porch, O noticed the stonework within it had been protected from the weather. The twin faces that peered down at them from their perch atop the sidelights were startlingly realistic. One of them wore glasses and bore a striking resemblance to the photo of Lawrence Linton she had seen. She wondered whether he had set his face here as a sort of signature. The other figure was a Green Man.

Emily rang the bell. The sound echoed inside the house. Blood trickled from the scratches on the back of her hand. She searched her pockets in vain for something to wipe it with.

"Do you have a hankie or something?" she asked. "I've cut myself."

"Oh, yes you have." O found a tissue in her pocket and handed it to her aunt as footsteps sounded from the far side of the door. An old woman opened it just wide enough to peer out at them.

"Miss Linton?"

"Yes."

"I'm Emily Endicott, and this is my niece, Ophelia. I've come to see the collection."

"Oh, yes, Miss Endicott. Please come in." And she

opened the door wide. "You must forgive me for being overly cautious, but I live alone here. And with this being the only house still inhabited on the street, I'm inclined to be a little nervous."

"I completely understand."

They stood in a long, high-ceilinged hall. O had never been in such a grand house. It was like something from another place and time.

"May I take your jacket?" Miss Linton said.

"Yes, thank you," said Emily. "My, what a lovely house."

Miss Linton hung her coat on a wooden rack, mounted below a mirror on the wall.

A wide staircase swept off to the upper floors. The stained-glass window on the landing spilled puddles of colored light on the polished stairs. A dark wooden rail curled down to a newel post carved in the shape of a sleeping dragon.

"Thank you. I'm afraid it's all a little much for me now. I had a housekeeper until about a year ago, but she had to leave. A death in the family. Please come this way, Miss Endicott, Ophelia." And she led them through a door that opened off the hall on the left.

"I'm afraid I'm a little late," said Emily. "My car wouldn't start."

"Don't fret about it, my dear. At my age, I've got nothing but time."

They entered a large circular room. In its day, it would have been a showpiece, a grand room for entertaining. Now, it seemed far too large for the few pieces of furniture it contained.

The walls were papered in a repeating pattern of flowers. Above a polished sideboard hung a large portrait in oil of a dignified middle-aged man seated on a chair, his hands folded in his lap. He looked vaguely troubled to be there, as though more pressing duties awaited him. He wore the same small round glasses as the sculpted figure on the front porch.

"My great-grandfather, the architect Lawrence Linton," said Miss Linton, when she noticed Emily studying the portrait.

"Yes. A very important man in the history of this community."

Miss Linton nodded, obviously pleased at the compliment. "Would you care to join me over here by the fire?" Four high-backed, red-velvet armchairs huddled around a vast fireplace on the far side of the room. She settled into one of them and motioned Emily and O to sit down opposite her.

A small oval table stood beside Miss Linton's chair, with a silver tea service and two cups and saucers. "Would you care for a cup of tea?" she asked.

"That would be very nice, thank you," said Emily.

O found it stifling this close to the fire. As Miss Linton went to get another cup from the sideboard, she shifted her chair a little farther back.

Miss Linton wore a dark silk dress, trimmed at the wrist and the neck with old lace. Her gray hair was drawn back into a bun. Her ruby earrings hung by her neck like bright drops of blood. She looked like someone who had gone astray in the centuries. In her prime, she would have been a beauty. Even now, something about her commanded attention.

"You will be wondering why I called you about the collection, rather than a large dealer or an appraiser," said Miss Linton, pouring the tea.

"As a matter of fact, I had wondered."

"Well, as I said on the phone, you came highly recommended by an old friend."

"May I ask who?"

"You may certainly ask, but I'm afraid I'm not at liberty to tell you. Suffice it to say that your paths have crossed in the past and he was impressed by you."

"I see."

There was something condescending in the woman's tone – a quiet but clear reminder that they were not of the same class.

"I was drawn by the name of your shop. I've always had a fascination for the Green Man, as did my great-grandfather. You can see several examples of the figure in the ornamentation on his buildings."

O remembered the sculpted figure above the sidelight at the front door.

"Was it you who named the shop?" asked Miss Linton.

"No," said Emily, "it's been a bookshop for many years. The original owner gave the shop its name."

"A very mysterious figure, the Green Man. I often wonder whether he is meant to be a symbol of good or of evil, an image of life or of death. The earliest examples are really quite frightening."

"Perhaps a little of both," said Emily. "He stands at the doorway between worlds. Life springs from him, all green and growing. But that life is rooted in darkness, as all life must be. And I imagine that, sometimes, a bit of the dark world crosses over."

19

The fire crackled in the grate. Emily sipped her tea. She felt hot and ill at ease. It was all she could do to sit quietly and keep up her end of the conversation. She put her cup down before it was finished and folded her hands on her lap. Red welts had risen around the scratches from the rosebush. Her hand throbbed, and she was feeling a little dizzy. The perfume the woman was wearing seemed suddenly overwhelming.

Finally, the conversation worked its way around to the collection. "It belonged originally to my great-grandfather," said Miss Linton. "He built this house and lived here until his death. The collection has grown over time. A while back, it outgrew the library where it is housed. I boxed some of the items and had them removed to the carriage house out back. My great-grandfather had rather unusual tastes, and I was happier without them in the house."

"I see," said Emily, sensing disaster. She cast a look at O.

"I will be moving in a little over a month," continued Miss Linton. "This place is more than I can manage now.

Even at the height of summer, there is a chill about it that seeps into my bones. I keep this fire going year-round – and still I am cold. The house and I are both too old. Our vital fires are burning low.

"I plan to move south – someplace hot, where I can sit in the sun all day and scorch. I intend to leave all this behind. It's of no use or interest to me anymore."

"What will happen to the house?"

"The others on the street are being demolished. The ground they are on is unstable. All of us here back onto a ravine, and over the years, erosion has undermined the foundations. I expect this house will suffer the same fate as the others."

"I'm sorry."

The woman dismissed the sentiment with a wave of her hand. The several large jeweled rings she wore hung slack on her thin fingers, sliding to the knuckles as her hands came to rest on the arms of her chair.

"You are interested in selling the entire collection, then?" said Emily, quietly steering the conversation back to her reason for being there.

"That is correct."

"Including the items in the carriage house?" she asked pointedly.

"Yes – I suppose so. Though I doubt any of *those* would be of much value."

"And has anyone else been to see the collection?"

"No, you are the first." With that, she pushed herself up out of her chair. "Now, if you're finished your tea, perhaps you would like to have a look at it."

Emily was glad to be free of the stifling room. She hooked her arm in O's as Miss Linton led them up the wide sweeping staircase to the second floor. They passed along a dim corridor, with doors opening on either side. She caught a glimpse into several high-ceilinged, shadow-hung rooms. It was exactly as she'd imagined it would be.

At the end of the corridor, they stopped at the foot of another staircase, this one steep and narrow. "Watch your step," said Miss Linton as they started up. When she opened the door at the top, light spilled down the stairs.

Emily and O followed the older woman into the room, and their mouths fell open.

It was a small circular room, perhaps twelve feet in diameter. Four tall lancet windows pierced the wall at regular intervals and filled the room with light. The walls between the windows were lined from floor to ceiling with books. One glance and Emily knew this was *it* – the collection she had long dreamt of discovering one day.

"I'll leave you to it, then," said Miss Linton. "You'll find me down by the fire when you're done."

"Thank you," said Emily in as even a tone as she could manage. She watched the woman cautiously descend the stairs. Then she closed the door quietly behind her, and they were alone.

"Do you believe this?" said O, looking around the room. "These books must be worth a fortune!"

Near the door, a fireplace was set in the wall. A table of the same dark wood as the shelves stood in the center of the room, with a chair drawn up to it. Emily put her bag down on the table and took out a notebook and pen.

Walking the circuit of the room, she scanned the shelves with increasing wonder, running her fingers along the spines of the books as if to assure herself they were real. It was a remarkable collection, the books as pristine as if they'd hatched there on the shelves. Books in lush Zaehnsdorf and Rivière bindings, the fine colored leathers still supple, the exquisite gilt stamping still radiant. There were rare first-edition, triple-volume novels of some of the brightest literary lights of the nineteenth century, several of them signed. A complete set of Dickens, its mottled boards still gleaming. A scarce copy of Keats' *Endymion*.

Along with these were older books, some dating as far back as the seventeenth century, their vellum bindings still white and supple, the type so crisp that it appeared to leap from the page – remarkably rare items she'd read about but never, in her wildest dreams, imagined she'd see.

"Well, I guess we should get to work," she said. "Let's start here by the window and work our way around. I'm going to need your help with the upper shelves." There was a ladder attached to a rail that ran around the circumference of the room. It had wheels on the bottom, like the one at the shop, and slid easily from section to section.

"Ready?" said Emily.

"Ready."

Beginning with the lower shelves, Emily worked her way methodically through the books, now and then plucking out a title for closer inspection, checking the title page and the verso, making notes in her little book. Occasionally, she set aside an item on the table.

When it came to the upper shelves, O would read out the titles and pass down items that Emily wanted to examine more closely. An hour and a half went by, and they had made it only a quarter of the way around the room. It was hot dusty work and, before long, they were both coughing like fiends.

Emily's hand throbbed. The welts had started to go down a little, but the scratches were red and sore. It reminded her of the time she'd stepped between two cats in a fight and been scratched for her pains. The back of her hand looked as if it been raked by claws. The mere sight of it made her feel queasy.

"Why don't you see if you can open a window, O? It's rather close in here."

The window, it seemed, had not been opened in some time and did its best to resist her efforts. Finally, it yielded with a groan, and fresh air rushed into the room. Emily and O stood together at the window, breathing it in.

The window overlooked the backyard of the house. In the foreground stood an old carriage house, blanketed in vines. The slate tiles on the roof were in disrepair. Several had broken away and lay like shattered teeth on the ground below. The whole scene spoke of ruin. Emily hated to imagine what the condition of the books stored in there would be. Behind the carriage house, the ground dropped away sharply. A tumbledown fence marked the boundary between the property and the wildness of the ravine beyond.

Turning from the window, Emily went back to work. She moved quickly now, realizing they would never finish otherwise. The highlight of the collection was a section of books on magic. They occupied one full bay, from floor to ceiling. O scrambled up the ladder to reach the higher shelves. Emily could not believe what she was seeing. There were titles here that had eluded her in all her years of collecting in the field.

Some of the books dated back to the beginning of the modern study of conjuring. There was a copy of Reginald Scot's *Discoverie of Witchcraft*, the first edition of 1584.

Almost all copies of the book had been burned by order of King James I. Yet here sat one that had been miraculously spared. There were mint copies of nineteenth-century conjuring classics: Robert-Houdin's *Secrets of Conjuring and Magic* and Professor Hoffman's *Modern Magic*, inscribed by the author to Linton. Along with these were a host of minor titles: books and pamphlets, how-to books of parlor magic and sleight of hand, rare ephemera she did not even know existed.

It was remarkable, like something from a dream. How could she even begin to place a value on such a collection? She wondered if Miss Linton had any idea how priceless it was. She suspected not. The woman seemed eager simply to have it off her hands.

Time flew by. Now and then as they worked, the stillness was broken by the cooing of pigeons and the restless beating of wings. Emily imagined they must be nesting under the eaves, outside the open window. Or perhaps they had found entrance into the roof above the room.

The sound grew louder as the light in the room grew dimmer. She took off her glasses. "I think we'd better go," she said, rubbing her eyes. "It's getting late, and I've got a pounding headache." There was a pile of perhaps two dozen books on the table in front of her.

"It's a truly magnificent collection, better than anything I've ever come across. I know a couple of collectors who will be very interested. I wonder exactly what was weeded from it and moved out back," she said, taking a final look out the window at the carriage house.

They packed up their things and made their way back through the large silent house to the ground floor. They found Miss Linton seated by the fire. She appeared to be asleep, but as Emily approached, she opened her eyes.

"I'm sorry to disturb you," said Emily.

"Nonsense. I was expecting you."

"We've gone through the collection quickly and singled out a few titles of special interest. I'd like to return and have a look at the items in the carriage house before I make an offer. I was wondering if I could drop by some-time tomorrow?"

Miss Linton assured her that there would be nothing worth her while in the carriage house, but agreed to let her have a look. She fetched Emily the key and asked her to return it through the mail slot when she was done.

By the time Emily and O had made the long trek back to the shop, they were both bone tired. O thoroughly washed the scratches on Emily's hand, spread anti-biotic cream on them, and wrapped the hand in a gauze bandage. Emily spent the better part of the next hour down in the shop, researching some of the items she'd seen that day, confirming all that she'd suspected about their rarity and value. Meanwhile, O prepared them something to eat.

Shortly after they finished, Emily said she was going to lie down for a bit. She dragged herself off to her room, lay down on the bed, and almost instantly fell asleep.

In the middle of the night, she woke with a start, utterly disoriented and bathed in sweat. She shed her clothes, pulled on her nightgown, and crawled back under the covers. As she was about to drift off, she noted in some dim corner of consciousness a smell of roses in the room.

Sleep brought with it the dream of the magic show.

20

All the time the magician had been performing, the mysterious box sat on the table at the center of the stage, commanding the attention of everyone in the room. Now he walked over to it and turned it slowly, so that they could see it on all sides.

"The curious symbols that cover the outside of this box are known as hieroglyphs," he said. "They are a form of writing used by the ancient Egyptians. The symbols were believed to possess magical powers. To safeguard that power, their meaning was kept hidden from all but a select few. So successfully was it hidden that their meaning has remained a mystery to this day.

"But why do these symbols appear on this box? What power might they impart to what lies within it? With the aid of a volunteer, Professor Mephisto will now share with you the secret of the Sphinx."

Child turned to child as the magician looked around the room, but none dared raise their hand. Finally his eyes fell on a girl sitting in the front row. He leaned over the edge of the stage and extended his hand to her.

"Come along now, my dear. I promise the professor won't bite."

At the urging of her friends, the girl put her hand in his and allowed herself to be led up onto the stage.

"Let's have a round of applause for the professor's assistant," he said as he guided the girl over to the table. "What is your name, my dear?"

"Ruby," she said.

"A lovely name. Now, Ruby, you will observe that the box is hinged at the front. I would like you to release the little catch you see there on the side and show our friends what the box contains." And he stepped aside.

As the girl released the catch, the front panel of the box swung open. A gasp went up from the crowd – for the box contained a woman's head.

She was wearing an Egyptian headdress, and her eyes were closed. Though it was certainly only a sculpted head, it was startlingly realistic, down to the delicate lashes on its eyelids and the faint flush on its cheeks. The sight of it struck fear in the hearts of the children, and a hush fell over the room.

"Now," said the magician to his assistant, "I would like you to walk all around the table. Look at it carefully from all sides. Pass your hand underneath it to assure our audience that there are no hidden panels, no cunningly angled mirrors, no deception of any kind."

The girl did as he asked, and, by the time she was done, it was clear to all that the little table concealed nothing.

"Now, Ruby, I want you to take this wand and, when I give you the signal, I would like you to tap it twice on the top of the box and say these words." And he bent down and whispered something in her ear. Then, handing her the wand, he retreated to the far side of the stage. He nodded to her, and she approached the box and tapped it twice.

"Sphinx, awake," she said in a trembling voice.

A tremor went through the head. Like someone waking from a long sleep, it slowly opened its eyes and moved them from side to side, surveying its surroundings.

On the magician's instructions, the girl asked the head to smile. It turned up the corners of its mouth in a grin that sent a shudder through the crowd. They knew this could not be a real head, but by what strange power was it able to look at them so and to smile in such a way?

From his post at the side of the stage, the magician also smiled. "Now, Ruby, why don't you ask our visitor some questions?" he said.

The girl was clearly frightened. It was all she could do to remain standing near the unnatural thing in the box. "I don't know what to ask it," she said nervously.

"Begin by asking its name."

She turned to the head in the box. "What is your name?"

Immediately, the head fastened its eyes on the girl, as though some dim flicker of life within it caught flame. Its eyes widened. Its mouth opened, and a voice issued from those parted lips, a voice unlike anything those in the room had ever heard before. It was deep and hollow – like something from beyond the grave.

"I am the Sphinx," it said.

"How old are you?" asked the girl at the magician's direction, for he now stood smiling by her side.

"Before your father's father and his father's father and his father's father were, I was," said the Sphinx.

The silence that had fallen over the room was broken by several older boys who sat together at the back, quietly snickering among themselves. They were old enough to know that a head in a box could not possibly talk. They were wise enough to know that the magician was throwing his voice to give the Sphinx the illusion of speech.

The professor looked directly at them. Turning to the girl, he whispered something in her ear. Then he walked over to the side of the stage and looked above him. Reaching up, he plucked a large orange from thin air, as if he had picked it from an invisible tree.

He stood calmly peeling the orange as the girl asked the Sphinx if it could recite a piece of poetry for them.

The Sphinx began to recite a long piece of verse. As it spoke, the magician stood quietly at the far side of the stage, eating the orange. He popped piece after piece into his mouth, until it was completely full of orange. It became clear to everyone, even the stubborn few who had doubted until then, that the magician was not throwing his voice. Somehow the head was thinking and speaking on its own.

As it finished reciting the poem, the Sphinx's powers seemed to wane. It closed its eyes and grew still. The magician approached the box and closed the front panel. Immediately, smoke billowed from it and tongues of flame crept from the cracks.

"What is life but a dream, death but a sleep from which we wake?" asked the magician as he reopened the panel.

The head had disappeared. Nothing remained but a mound of ashes in the bottom of the box.

21

The following day, armed with the key Miss Linton had given her, Emily made a visit to the tumble-down carriage house. Her hand was feeling better after O had bathed it in salt water that morning and redressed it. Over the girl's protests, Emily had left her behind to mind the shop, assuring her she would be fine to look over the books on her own. The car, taking pity on her condition, started on the first try.

As she tramped through the long grass toward the carriage house, the pigeons sitting on the roof took flight with a startled flurry. She watched them whirl through the air, settling finally on the turret of the house, where the library was housed. Snapping off the spindly green creepers that had grown across the door, Emily turned the key in the rusted lock.

There was a dank, shut-in smell about the place. She flicked the light switch inside the door and a dim bulb dangling from the beams winked into life. Weaving through the clutter of abandoned furniture and rusted gardening tools, she discovered two small wooden crates tucked against the far wall. A smell of mildew and damp drifted out when she opened the lids.

The crates were piled high with books. She lifted an old calfskin-covered book and gave it a sniff. Why on earth would Lenora Linton put these things out here? she wondered as she carefully opened the old volume. She rooted through the piles, stacking the books carefully on the inside of the lids on the floor beside her.

Most of the books were not in English. Her Latin was rusty, her German patchy, her Hebrew nonexistent. From what she could decipher, the books explored arcane and esoteric byways of thought – books of magic and mysticism that, in an earlier age, it might have been dangerous to own. Damaged though they were, she was stunned to come upon such a find.

The dim, web-hung place was beginning to give her the creeps. She carefully repacked the crates, locked the door, and put the key through the mail slot out front.

Over the next several days, Emily sought advice from fellow dealers on the more valuable items in the Linton collection. Armed with that, she put together what seemed a most generous offer and went to the bank to arrange for a line of credit. It was necessary to put the shop up as collateral, but she felt it well worth the risk. At the end of the week, she contacted Lenora Linton. Miss Linton seemed pleased with the offer but said she would need to consult her lawyer. She assured Emily it was a mere formality.

However, when she'd still had no word by the middle of the next week, Emily began to fear that something had gone wrong. Perhaps the size of the offer had led Miss Linton to believe that the collection might be worth even more. Perhaps she had decided to contact one of the larger auction houses, after all.

Meanwhile, O busied herself with preparations for the poetry reading on the following Tuesday. It was to be something of a trial run, so she wanted as many people as possible to turn out. She printed a flyer and made a sweep of the neighborhood, taping it to lampposts, posting it on the cluttered board at the back of the coin laundry. Gigi agreed to put one in the window of her shop.

The Mind Spider's window, which parents whisked their curious children past, was already chock full of close-up photos of Tiny's work displayed on various body parts. Still, he took a few flyers off her hands and said he would talk it up with his customers.

While she was making the rounds, O mailed a letter she'd written to her father. In it, she mentioned meeting Leonard Wellman and learning about the Tuesdays at the Green Man. She talked about Emily's decision to start up the poetry readings again, with her help. She even divulged that she'd been doing a little writing herself and decided at the last minute to include a copy of the poem she'd written on the rooftop:

> Perched high on the rooftop
> I am level with treetops,
> Kin to windblown branches,
> Neighbor to clouds.
> Twilight falls,
> Birds clamor among the leaves,
> Call down the dark,
> Coax stars from hiding.
> Below me, night spreads
> Its crazy quilt –
> Patchwork houses, roof
> Stitched seamlessly to roof,
> Treetop to treetop,
> Quilted with threads of light.

She returned to the Green Man full of news. "You won't believe who agreed to take a pile of flyers for the reading," she said as she came into the shop and dropped the remainder on the ledge by the door.

There was no answer; Emily was not at the desk. She found her in the back room on the couch. One look and O knew something was wrong.

"What is it?"

"I got a call from Lenora Linton. There's a problem."

"What sort of problem?"

"Another dealer has made a counter offer. Her lawyer has advised her to accept it."

"I thought you said she hadn't told anyone else about the collection."

"She still claims she hasn't. Who knows, maybe it was one of the dealers I spoke to about pricing a couple of the items."

"That's a little underhanded."

"If that's what happened. But I seriously can't think of anyone I spoke to who would do something like that. Anyway, I think Miss Linton feels badly about it. She's offered us the items in the carriage house for next to nothing. I'm sure there's some valuable material there. It's beyond my expertise, and I'm not sure I'll be able to sell it in the condition it's in. But if we turn it down, I'm afraid the whole lot will just wind up in the garbage when she moves."

That evening, Emily phoned Lenora Linton and agreed to her offer for the carriage-house books. On Friday, she went with Miles and picked them up. They put them in the back room of the shop beside the couch. You noticed their musty smell immediately on entering the room.

22

When O woke up, it was already stifling in the attic room. The curtains glowed like a fire in a grate. The fan swiveled back and forth on top of the dresser, blowing the heat around. At the end of each sweep, it gave a petulant little click, just to let you know it wasn't happy with its lot in life.

She lay listening to it, getting her bearings before she ventured out of bed. It was Saturday morning. The poetry reading was scheduled for the following Tuesday, July 14. That would make today – she counted backwards in her head – July 11. Since all the calendars in the shop and the flat had mysteriously disappeared, it was a bit of an adventure keeping dates straight. When she'd asked Emily about the disappearing calendars, her aunt just shrugged it off.

She went to the window now and opened the curtains. One of the chairs seemed slightly out of place. It wasn't the first time she'd noticed that. She told herself it must have been the wind.

By the time she'd made the bed and thrown on her

clothes, the sweat was streaming down her face. She retreated to the second floor.

Normally, Emily would be sitting bleary-eyed at the kitchen table, cradling a cup of coffee and listening to the radio. They would mutter a brief "good morning," and O would fix herself some breakfast and coax Emily into eating a slice of toast or a bowl of oatmeal. At ten, they would head downstairs to open the shop for the day.

But when she came downstairs this morning, she found the kitchen empty and the kettle cold. "Aunt Emily?" she called down the hall and waited for the stock response – "If you keep calling me that, I swear I'll scream." But there was silence.

"Emily?" Louder this time. "Are you there?" A quaver of unease had crept into her voice.

She padded down the book-lined hall, peeking first into the living room, then into Emily's bedroom and the bathroom they shared. Finally, she walked along to her aunt's workroom at the end of the hall.

The door was open and the room empty, which was extremely uncharacteristic of Emily, who normally locked the room when she wasn't using it. This was in response to an incident in the distant past. One of the regulars around the shop at the time, a fellow poet, had been allowed to use the washroom upstairs and had taken the liberty of nosing around in her workroom.

Emily was extremely secretive about her work. "Don't tell me about it," she said, when O began to tell her an idea she had for a poem. "Don't say a word. Just write it and then show it to me. If you talk about it first, you'll kill it for sure."

O ventured into the forbidden room. The clutter that had flourished in the shop and found its way up to the flat stopped abruptly at the door. The room was as spare as a monk's cell. A large oak desk sat in the center, the rug around it worn threadbare. A simple cot, with a blanket folded neatly at the foot, was pushed against one wall. Books and manuscripts were ranged neatly on a set of unfinished shelves. A bulletin board – bristling with scraps of paper, found objects, and photos – was the only thing to break the bare expanse of wall. She noticed a recent photo of herself among them, half-hidden by a dried rose hanging upside down from a length of dusty thread.

Though the sun streamed through the window, the desk lamp was on. It shone down on an old typewriter, with a sheet of paper rolled in it that appeared to be the draft of a poem. O leaned down to look. The same few lines had been typed once, corrected by hand, and typed again beneath:

> *Things I thought long past*
> *Grow present once again.*
> *I see your soundless eyes*

As I saw them then.
Your shrouded voice shakes off
The dust of years,
Leans low and whispers
In my ear.

The words sent a chill through her. She switched off the lamp and hurried back along the hall. Fighting a sudden surge of panic, she opened the door to the shop and made her way down the dim stairs.

As she opened the door at the bottom, she heard Emily's voice. It was coming from the back room of the shop. It seemed someone was there with her.

"You were always good with languages," she heard. "Can you make head or tail of this? It's some kind of Hebrew text."

O found her aunt sitting on the couch. One of the boxes of carriage-house books stood open on the floor in front of her, spilling its musty perfume into the room. Several large old books were piled on the floor beside it. One lay open on her lap.

Emily was alone.

It wasn't the first time this had happened. On a couple of other occasions, O had come upon Emily unawares and discovered her deep in conversation – with no one. On the mad-poet scale of one to ten, it was a solid nine.

She coughed to let her presence be known. Emily jumped, and the book fell from her lap.

"Good Lord, O. You nearly frightened me to death."

"I'm sorry. I was worried when I didn't find you upstairs."

"I woke up early, so I decided to come down and take a run at this before we opened. It's a collection of Hermetic texts from the late Renaissance. These writers were all seeking to gain spiritual power by magical means. They believed everything was impregnated with a hidden divine life. Through the knowledge of true magic, they felt they could release the spiritual power within things and overcome the forces of darkness in the world.

"There are early editions of the *Corpus Hermeticum*, Bruno's *De Magia*, works by Agrippa, Robert Fludd, Tommaso Campanella – fascinating, rare material, and I've barely scraped the surface; also a number of books in Hebrew, which, I suspect, are cabalistic texts. My friend Isaac Steiner teaches at the university and is an expert in the field. I'm sure he'd be eager to see this."

O noticed a book with red leather binding sitting on the arm of the couch, the letters *L.L.* stamped in gold on the cover. She picked it up.

"What's this?" she asked.

"It was in with the rest of this stuff. It seems to be a journal, most likely Linton's. His initials are on the cover. But take a look inside."

O fanned to a random page. The ink had turned a rusty brown. She tried to read the cramped, spidery handwriting. "It's in another language," she said.

"Yes. Hebrew."

"Why would he write it in Hebrew?"

"Perhaps to keep it from prying eyes."

"But why?"

"Your guess is as good as mine," Emily said.

At ten o'clock, O turned the sign in the window, opened the front door, and dragged out the bargain bins. She rolled down the awning to keep off the morning sun. It was going to be a scorcher.

When she switched on the radio, the announcer was introducing a Lester Young number, "Lester Leaps In." Emily's voice boomed from the back room, "Turn that up!"

Lester was one of her aunt's favorite jazz artists. He was the original hipster, the ultimate in cool. He spoke in a clipped, cryptic slang he had invented, wore his porkpie hat perched at a rakish angle, and held his sax sideways when he played. The Beat Poets of the 1950s embraced him as one of their own and used to compose poetry to his music.

While Lester played, O shelved the pile of books Emily had left for her. She was beginning to see a connection between jazz players and poets. They were both a little odd, outsiders and rebels exercising a sort of passive resistance to society at-large, dedicated to expressing their unique gifts in their own way.

A few browsers wandered in. She sold a couple of books, made note of them in the log, and directed people to sections they inquired about. Business was picking up. Meanwhile, Emily continued working in the back room.

Around noon, the bell rang and O looked up. The dark-haired boy with the light fingers walked into the shop. He worked his way over to the poetry section. She noticed a couple of burrs stuck to the back of his sleeve, a couple more to the cuff of his pants.

She waited to see if he was going to take another book, unsure of what she would do if he did. Instead, he reached into his pocket, pulled out a book, and placed it on the shelf.

Emily came out from the back room with something she wanted to show O. She noticed the boy browsing through the poetry section and watched him for a minute, then wandered back into the rear room. No sooner had she disappeared through the doorway than the boy seized his opportunity. He reached out, slid another book into his coat, and made his way quickly out of the shop.

Okay – so he wasn't a book *thief*. He was a book *borrower*. The Green Man was just his local library. O glanced up in the mirror. Emily was making notes on a pad of paper balanced on the arm of the couch and appeared lost to the world.

O got up and headed over to the poetry section. She pulled out the book she had seen the boy return to the shelf. It was a collection of Edgar Allan Poe. She carried it back to the desk to take a closer look.

Poe was one of her personal favorites – one of the poets whose work her father used to leave lying around the house for her to discover. There was a strange beauty to his poetry, a sense of the nearness of the supernatural. So her mystery boy liked Poe too. He instantly went up a few notches in her estimation.

She leafed through the book. There were no markings, no signs of abuse. As she fanned through to the back, a piece of pale blue paper fluttered out. It had been folded twice. She unfolded it and found a poem written on it. She thought, at first, it might be a transcription of one of Poe's, but as she read it through, she realized it was not.

There was no telling how long it had been in the book, but it didn't have the faded look of old writing. Maybe it was the work of her mysterious stranger. So he was a poet. He shot up several more notches.

At that moment Emily reappeared with a book she wanted to look up in one of her reference books on the desk. O tucked the poem back inside the book. She was tempted to show it to Emily, but there was no way of doing that without going through the whole story. And she would rather keep her stranger's secrets to herself for now.

Emily put her book down on the corner of the desk and reached for the heavy old copy of *The American Bookman*. She started searching through the index. "Have you seen that boy before?" she asked, without looking up.

"What boy?"

"The one who was just in here."

"Yes, he's been in before when I was here alone."

"Did he buy anything?"

"No, just browsing."

"He reminds me a little of Arthur Rimbaud."

"Who is that?"

"A French poet. Here, I'll show you." And she walked O down to a space on the wall near the front of the shop, where there was a picture of a group of men gathered at a table. She pointed to one, a boy who sat resting his head on his hand. He was much younger than the others.

"That's Rimbaud. He was just sixteen when he appeared on the scene. Brash and outrageous, he turned the polite world of French poetry on its ear. But he was a genius. He wrote poetry as if he were making magic. Then, before he turned twenty, he abandoned writing completely and went off to Africa."

She wandered into the back room, leaving O staring at the boy in the painting. He did look a little like the boy in the shop.

That night, O took the collection of Poe's poetry upstairs with her. She read the poem tucked inside it over again. If the poem was his, he would probably miss it sooner or later and come back to retrieve it. She decided to tuck it back in the book and reshelve it first thing in the morning.

23

On the morning of the reading, Emily repacked the carriage-house collection into smaller boxes for O to cart upstairs, where they would be out of the way. Then she phoned her friend Isaac Steiner and arranged for him to come over that weekend to take a look at several items of possible interest.

O spent the morning sprucing up the reading room. She swept the floor, sneezed, dusted the shelves, sneezed, vacuumed Psycho's fur off the old couch, sponged down the grungy spots, and strategically placed pillows to hide the tears in the upholstery. She unfolded a dozen chairs stacked against the wall and set them in two shallow rows. It would be the first poetry reading she'd ever attended, and she was excited.

Her excitement helped to alleviate her disappointment that Rimbaud had not returned to retrieve his poem from the Poe collection. She wondered when she would see him again. This time, she was determined to talk to him.

The weather threatened, and business was slow. There

were ominous rumblings in the distance. They decided to close early. Suddenly, the sky opened and it poured. O rushed out to rescue the bargain books, turned the sign in the window, and locked the door.

The meeting was scheduled for eight o'clock. That left them time to put together a quick supper and make any last-minute preparations. She was a bundle of nerves. Emily assured her it would just be a small affair – a few regulars O had seen around the shop and perhaps a couple of curious newcomers who'd seen the flyers she'd distributed around the neighborhood.

After dinner she went up and changed, put a clip in her hair, and pinched some color into her cheeks. At seven she headed downstairs.

Emily had brought out the large coffee percolator she used for the readings. O rinsed it and measured in the water and coffee. She sat it on a table covered with a clean cloth from upstairs. Alongside the coffeepot she set a carton of cream, a bowl of sugar cubes, some spoons from the kitchen drawer, and two tall spires of overturned Styrofoam cups.

She opened the pack of chocolate chip cookies she'd bought and put some on a plate. Then she made a sign suggesting a donation of fifty cents for a cup of coffee and a cookie, and leaned it against an empty jar on the table.

The rain was still coming down fairly hard. She was beginning to worry that no one would show up and the whole thing would be a dismal failure, when the first arrivals came straggling through the door with dripping umbrellas.

Over the next half hour, a steady trickle of people made their way through the shop and into the back room. They stood around talking and eating enough of the cookies that O finally spirited them away so there would be some left for the break.

Poets, it appeared, came in all forms: young and old, made-up and rumpled, soft-voiced and loud, modern and traditional, stout and lean. The wonder of it was you could have passed almost any of them on the street and never have suspected they were poets. They made a virtue of invisibility.

She recognized some as regulars at the shop, friends who would stop by to chat with Emily. Leonard Wellman and Miles were there. Tiny from the Mind Spider Tattoo Parlor came with a couple of his friends. Most people seemed to know one another. A couple of newcomers hung around the fringes, cradling their coffees and scanning the spines of the books on the shelves. Someone's rose perfume wafted in the air.

As O glanced around the room, she noticed someone leaning against a wall of books in the corner. He held a silver-handled cane in one hand and a black felt hat in the other. With his deep-set eyes and his little clipped goatee, he looked enough like Ezra Pound to be his twin. And a woman who sat with her cup on her lap and a large hat on her head reminded O of the portrait of Marianne Moore that hung near the poetry section. She was tempted to run to the front of the shop and see if some of the frames on the wall were empty, their subjects having quietly slipped out to attend the reading.

At eight Emily rang a little brass bell, in the shape of a woman with a hoop skirt, and brought the meeting to order. The mutter of conversation died down as people took their seats. Considering the short notice and the stormy night, it was a decent turnout. Over a dozen people were in the room.

"I'm so glad you took the trouble to come out in such nasty weather," said Emily. "It's nice to see some familiar faces and to renew acquaintances. And, as always, we welcome those who are here for the first time.

"The Tuesdays have been an institution at the Green Man for a good many years, as most of you know. For the past few months, ill health has forced me to suspend our meetings. I have missed them, and especially the companionship of fellow poets. I would like to thank my niece, Ophelia Endicott, for helping to get them going again." O could feel her face redden.

"Writing poetry is a solitary profession. We work alone – alone with words. Sometimes those words are as warm and welcoming as lovers, at others as chill and remote as the moon. We come here like travelers returned from our solitary explorations, armed with the log of the journey and with an eagerness to share. That is the purpose of this meeting.

"The rules, such as they are, are simple. There is no sign-up sheet, no drawing of lots. We rely on a combination of courage and inspiration. If you have something you would like to share, we invite you to come to the front, state your name, and read. Please speak slowly, but loud enough that those of us with aging ears can hear. We ask that you do not go on for more than ten minutes.

"If you have written the next *Paradise Lost*, this is not the place to air that. You may, if you chose, share a small portion of your paradise – enough to whet our appetite. If you go on for too long, I will ring the little bell lady. Now, that's quite enough from me. It's your turn."

There was a warm round of applause as Emily returned to her seat. O found it remarkable to see her aunt in such a setting. Here was someone different from the woman who sat across the kitchen table from her each day, who ruled quietly over her domain of books from behind the cluttered desk in the shop. Here was Emily in an entirely new element, where she was strong and forceful and honored among fellow poets.

Thin sheaves of paper had miraculously appeared from

pockets and purses. As she panned the room to see who would be the first brave soul to fill the silence, O caught a fleeting glimpse of someone she hadn't seen – a dark figure merged in the shadows on the far side of the room. There was something vaguely unsettling about him. But when she looked again a minute later, he was gone.

A woman with short gray hair stood and made her way to the front. O had seen her talking to Emily before the reading began.

"Hello, my name is Elizabeth Redshaw, and I am very pleased to be here. I think I echo everyone's sentiments when I say how delighted I am that the Tuesdays have resumed. Tonight I would like to share with you a piece I have written. It's called 'A Scent of Eden.'" And she began to read.

O had stationed herself on a chair at the entrance to the room, where she could keep an ear open for any latecomers. Before the meeting started, she had locked the door and switched off the lights out front so that people walking by wouldn't think the shop was open for business. Suddenly, she heard a light rap on the door. She peered through the shadows but saw no sign of anyone out there in the dark. She imagined it must have been the wind and turned back to the room. Elizabeth Redshaw had finished reading her poem. The polite round of applause was cut short as she launched into another.

Again, there came a faint rapping. This time O rose from her chair and walked through the darkened shop. The rain had started up again in earnest, pelting heavily against the plate-glass window. Perhaps *that* was what she'd heard.

But as she peered past the PLEASE KNOCK FOR POETRY READING sign she'd hung in the door, she saw someone huddled under the overhang, with his back to her. She undid the latch and opened the door.

The figure turned. It was the boy in black – the book borrower. He was soaked to the skin. His collar was turned up, and his hair ran with rainwater.

"Oh my God!" she said. "How long have you been standing there?"

"Not long."

"I'm afraid we're closed."

"Oh. I guess I have the wrong night."

"Oh, you're here for the poetry reading? Of course you are. No, this is the right night. I'm sorry, come in, please. It's just in the back there."

While she locked up again, the boy headed to the room. He stood dripping in the doorway.

Elizabeth Redshaw was still reading. Emily's hand kept reaching for the little brass lady, then dropping back to the arm of the chair. Finally, the reader finished. There was a round of applause as she returned to her seat.

Again there was a rustling of papers, a panning of eyes

around the room. The tall rumpled guy who had come with Tiny went up to the front. His kinky red hair fell to his shoulders, and he had tattoos up both arms.

He pulled a sheaf of tattered papers from his pocket.

"Hi," he said. "I'm Jasper Cook." And, without further ado, he started to read. His poetry was full of extravagant noises, extended silences, chants and yowls. He clapped his hands, stamped his feet, shook his curly head. It was unlike anything O had ever seen.

People weren't quite sure how to respond. They turned to one another and smiled nervously. Finally, Tiny broke into a laugh. The crowd quickly relaxed and got into the swing of it.

Through it all, Rimbaud stood dripping in the doorway. O noticed Emily looking over at her and raising an eyebrow. Her aunt scrawled something on a scrap of paper and passed it back.

Get that boy a towel, it read.

O raced upstairs and returned with a clean towel. "I thought you might like to dry yourself off a little," she said.

"Thanks." He wiped his face and toweled his hair lightly, leaving the towel resting around his neck. There was a pool of water on the floor, but he didn't seem to notice.

He was completely enraptured by Jasper Cook's performance. He closed his eyes, moved his head from side to side, and smiled to himself.

As she stood there beside him, O had a chance to observe him – the fine delicate features, the almost ivory-like skin. When he smiled, there was a devilish edge to his grin, and something kindled in the depths of those dark eyes. She was glad he had her towel around his neck.

A couple of others got up, read, sat down. She didn't notice what they read. Finally, the group broke for coffee. People milled about. Make conversation, she told herself.

"Have you been to a reading before?" she asked as she brought out the cookie plate.

"No, I'm new to town."

"I've seen you in the shop," she said. They traded glances. She offered him a cookie. He took two.

"My aunt says you look like Rimbaud. Do you know Rimbaud?"

"Yes, I know him. Now, if I could only write like him . . ."

"I think you write very well." The words were out before she realized what she'd said. "I think I'll get a coffee." And a knife to slit my throat, she thought.

She poured two coffees, but by the time she got back, he was gone. The towel was draped over the back of a chair. She was sure he had fled, but then she heard a noise coming from the shop. He was standing in the shadows by the front window, looking out into the night.

"I got a coffee for you."

"Thanks," he said, taking the cup from her. After a

long silence, he asked, "How do you know that I write?"

"You left a poem in the Poe collection."

"I see."

He followed her as she walked over to the poetry section and pulled the Poe off the shelf, opening it to reveal the folded piece of pale blue paper.

"I left it in there for you," she said. "I thought you might come back for it." She handed it to him. "It *is* yours, isn't it?"

"Yeah, it's mine. I hope I'm a better poet than I am a thief. Look, I'm sorry. Like I said, I'm new to town. And I'm . . . a little short of money."

"It's okay. I mean, it could have been worse, right? You could actually have stolen the book."

"I wouldn't do that."

"I figured that."

"What's your name?" he asked.

"O."

"O. Like the letter?"

"That's right."

"I like that."

"Thanks. What's yours?"

He paused for a moment. "I kind of like 'Rimbaud,' actually."

"Fine. Look, I should get back. I'm supposed to be helping out." She turned to go.

"Wait," he said, holding out the poem to her. "Please – take it. And thanks."

She escaped to the other room and gathered up the empty cups while her aunt held court. In a few minutes, the second half started. Every now and then, she would glance over at the patch of wetness on the floor. There was no other sign of him. He had slipped off quietly into the night.

Before she climbed into bed, O took out the folded piece of pale blue paper and read the poem again:

> In dark of night, I spin this dream of flesh,
> Shape bone from woven branches,
> Draw blood from the sap of sleeping trees,
> Fashion skin from thick veined leaves.
> For eyes, I seek out fallen stars,
> For ears, scoop shells from the sounding sea,
> For mouth, I rout the squirrel from its hollow,
> For breath, snare the wind that whispers in the trees.

Tucking the poem safely away in her journal, she switched off the light and fell asleep to the patter of rain on the roof.

24

The morning after the meeting, Emily left after breakfast to see Leonard Wellman. At ten, O went down to open the shop. She unlocked the front door and pulled out the bargain bins. The street was still damp from last night's rain. She looked up and down it, hoping Rimbaud might be there.

She spent most of her time these days thinking about him. Yet she didn't even know his real name, only the one they'd given him – and he'd willingly taken. He said he was new to town and didn't have much money. So where was he living? How did he eat? She remembered the figure rooting through the containers behind the bakery that night.

It had been too late to do much cleaning up after the reading. Now she dumped the dregs of the coffee down the sink and rinsed out the percolator. She cleaned the table, folded the chairs, and returned them to their place against the wall.

The visitors had taken down some books from the shelves, which she returned to their places. As she was putting a book on stage magic back in its spot, she noticed a folded sheet of paper tucked in the space where it was to go. She slid it out.

The paper was yellow with age, and as she opened it, a small corner piece flaked off in her hand. It seemed to be an old playbill for a magic show:

<u>PROFESSOR MEPHISTO PRESENTS</u>
An Evening of Magic and Mystery
Consisting of
Wonderful Illusions, Startling Feats,
And Astonishing Transformations
NEVER BEFORE WITNESSED.
Among the features will be found
The following wondrous acts:
THE MYSTERY OF THE
CHARMED CHEST
THE AMAZING AUTOMATON
And his
ENCHANTED CARDS
The Seeming Miracle of
THE MYSTIC MIRROR
The Awe-Inspiring Phenomenon of
THE SPHINX
The Incomprehensible Marvel of
THE INDIAN BASKET

Not for the faint of heart.
THE ETHEREAL SUSPENSION
In which a child will sleep in the air.
And concluding with the justly famous
HUMAN SALAMANDER
In which the Professor will master
The might of fire.
<u>ONE NIGHT ONLY</u>
Saturday, August 8th
The Professor's book, revealing the secrets
Of his Magic Art, will be presented
To all volunteers from the audience.
SHOW BEGINS AT EIGHT

O was sure it must be valuable. She carefully flattened it and put it inside a plastic cover, as she had seen Emily do with other valuable paper ephemera that came across her desk. She set it aside to show her later.

That night at dinner, she brought it out.

"Emily, I found something today I thought you might be interested in." She was sure her aunt would be surprised by it and hoped to be praised for protecting it properly. She handed it to her and waited for her reaction.

Emily took it quite cheerfully and began to read. But, almost immediately, a change came over her. The color drained from her face. Her hands began to tremble, and the playbill fell to the table.

"Emily, what's the matter?"

Her aunt stared through her as if she were not there. She had gone as rigid as stone. Through a fog of panic, O remembered the tiny pills her aunt always carried with her. She reached into Emily's sweater pocket and found them. Taking one out, she forced it under her aunt's tongue.

"Don't swallow it. Just keep it there," she said.

Within a minute, the color crept back into Emily's face. The rigor that had gripped her began to relax. The distance in her eyes disappeared, and she was back in the room with her again, looking dazed. O had never been happier to see anyone in her life. She threw her arms around Emily's neck and started to cry.

"Oh my God, Emily. Do you want me to call your doctor?"

"No. I just need to lie down for a minute." Her voice was as brittle as the playbill.

O cleared the couch in the living room and settled her on it, a pillow under her head. Emily assured her she was feeling all right and didn't want to hear any talk about doctors. But she *would* like a cup of tea.

As O was gathering the tea things together, she glanced down at the playbill. It had aged noticeably since she first saw it that morning.

She told herself to be calm, but still the cups rattled on the tray like chattering teeth as she carried the tea things into the living room. She poured a cup for both of them.

"Thank you, dear," said Emily, cradling the cup in her hands as she took a sip. "Do you know what I'd like more than anything in the world right now?"

"I think so," said O. "Where are they?"

"In my jacket pocket."

O disappeared down the hall and returned with Emily's cigarettes and lighter. Emily shook one loose, lit it, and inhaled deeply.

"That's better. I promise you, I'll be good again tomorrow. But, for the moment, I desperately need to be bad."

She calmed noticeably as the tea in the cup disappeared and the cigarette was smoked down to a stub. She butted it in the ashtray that had briefly become a candy dish. The candies lay strewn on the table beside it.

"Now, tell me exactly where you found that playbill."

"I was cleaning up the reading room this morning, after last night. Someone had taken a book down from the magic section, and, when I went to return it, the playbill was sitting in the empty spot on the shelf."

"So either it had been there between the books all the time, or someone at the meeting put it there."

"What is it?"

"A memory. A memory – and perhaps a warning of things to come. I have something to tell you, O. Something I should have told you some time ago. I warn you, by the end of it you may doubt my sanity – if you don't already. But I swear every word of it is true.

"When your father first approached me with the idea of your coming to stay for the summer, I delayed a long time before answering him. I was full of doubts. I was still full of doubts when I finally did agree.

"You see, this year marks an anniversary of sorts – an anniversary of something that happened long ago. I successfully buried the memory of it for many years. I buried it under a mound of books – under a mound of books and poems. And, over time, I tramped the ground down hard over it. So hard that I hoped it would stay buried.

"But I can feel it coming all the same. Everything I write these days is about it. I've removed every calendar in the place, so I wouldn't constantly be thinking about it, constantly counting down the days."

So that was why all the calendars had suddenly disappeared, thought O, as she watched her aunt pour more tea and reach for another cigarette. Her stomach was in knots – but, this time, it was not the cigarette smoke. It was something in her aunt's voice – an undertone of muted terror she had never heard before. Emily lit her cigarette.

"It's not just houses that can be haunted. People can be haunted too. *I* am haunted – haunted by something that happened a lifetime ago."

25

"I was fourteen at the time. Already I had dreams of becoming a poet. Already I had felt the wonderful magic of creating something new with words. And by some strange irony, I was introduced to another, darker magic at just that moment. I wonder now whether it was mere coincidence, or whether the very gift that opens one to the light might also attune one to the workings of the dark. That's why I warned you that poetry can be a dangerous thing.

"It all unfolded during the long sweltering summer following my graduation from grade school. My teacher that year was Miss Potts. She was a small, strange, slightly bewildered older woman with a passion for poetry, and it proved infectious. She was near retirement. I can see now that the prospect of it must have appalled her. She clung to teaching like I cling to this shop – because she knew nothing could fill the chasm that losing it would leave.

"In my mind, she's always dear old Miss Potts, and I'm the age I was when we first met. But, in fact, she's long gone, and I'm older than she was then. And here I am now, about to tell you the very story she told me.

"School had been out for less than a month when I received a phone call from Miss Potts. She asked me about something she'd found in my desk while she was cleaning out the classroom for the summer – an old play-bill for a magic show. A playbill much like the one you found this morning.

"As it happened, I *had* seen it. It appeared on my desk on the last day of class. During all the confusion of that day, it somehow got pushed to the back of the desk, which is where she found it. She was excited – *relieved* is perhaps a better word – that I'd seen it, and asked if we could meet. She didn't want to talk about it over the phone.

"We arranged to meet in a park. I was baby-sitting my little brother Albert, who was just a toddler then. She had the playbill with her. When she showed it to me, I told her it was the one I'd seen. I think she was hoping that meeting with me might somehow shed light on the mystery of its sudden appearance. But I had no more idea where it had come from than she did.

"For whatever reason – and it may simply have been because she sensed a kindred spirit in me – she sat beside me on the bench and proceeded to tell me the most incredible story I had ever heard.

"It was about a magic show she had attended as a child and a magician of such incredible power that, even after all those years, it was impossible for her to forget him.

"The show took place on a hot August night. A boy had pasted a flyer for it to the pole in front of her house. A traveling magician was passing through town and was to give a show at the Caledon depot for one night only. She begged her parents to let her go and, finally, they agreed.

"Her father accompanied her, as did several other parents. But the magician no sooner appeared onstage than he asked them all to leave. This was to be a children's show. Well, leave they did, though not without some misgivings. For they must have sensed that this was no ordinary magician.

"There was something in his voice, she said . . . something in his eyes – a power. He performed incredible feats with such ease that he seemed more than human. To look in his eyes was to become lost in them, utterly and willingly lost.

"He seemed to know the secret wish of every child there and to possess the power to grant it. Within the confines of that room, all things seemed possible – to fly, to disappear, to bring things into being with the wave of a hand.

"His words were sweet as honey, his voice melodious as music. When he spoke, it was as if every word was meant for her alone. But, despite it all, something kept catching in her mind – a doubt that drew her back each time she felt herself about to fall hopelessly under his spell.

"It was more a feeling than a thought. Like a gust of wind parting the painted backdrop of a play, for a moment the magic would fail and something would show itself behind the smooth allure – something with neither blood nor heart nor human feeling. Something of blind implacable power. For an instant it was there – and then it was gone.

"His hooded eyes would flare and there would be a momentary ferocity. The winning smile would flicker and there would be a sudden glint of fang. The melodious voice would falter and, in its place, there would be the sharp bark of command.

"Behind it all, she sensed an insatiable hunger – a desire to possess her wholly, to hollow her out until she was no more than an empty shell. And then it would pass, and again there would be only the wonder.

"Several times during the performance, the magician asked for a volunteer from the audience to assist in an illusion. Everyone who volunteered received a copy of his little book, which he said contained the secrets of his magic art.

"The highlight of the show was an illusion called the Decollation of John the Baptist. The magician called for a volunteer, and a boy went up. He had the boy lie down on a table and covered his head with a cloth. Producing a long-bladed knife, he reached under the cloth and, with one quick downward motion, buried the blade in the wood of the table. He picked up the cloth and what it contained and carried it to the foot of the table. With a flick of the wrist, he whisked the cloth away.

"There stood the boy's severed head. Slowly it opened its eyes. The magician asked it questions, and the head answered back. After a while, the magician covered the head with the cloth again and returned it to the body. He spoke some magical words. A tremor went through the boy and he sat up, rubbing his neck. The audience applauded wildly. Clutching his copy of the little book, the boy returned to his seat, apparently none the worse for his experience.

"However, later that year, the same boy was involved in a fatal accident. He was crossing a railway bridge, when suddenly he looked back and began to run furiously for the other side. He had almost reached safety, when he looked back once more and suddenly leapt from the bridge, plunging into the ravine far below. They found him there later, dead of a broken neck. A group of boys who had witnessed the tragedy said it appeared the boy had spotted an oncoming train as he was crossing the bridge. But there was no train.

"No one connected the two incidents at the time. But Miss Potts became convinced that, long before the fall, the boy had already died. She believed he had died up there on that stage three months before.

"As for the magician, he vanished without a trace. The room he had rented above the depot was empty. The food that had been brought to him sat untouched. The bed showed no sign of ever having been slept in.

"The memory of the magician and that fateful show stayed with her through the years. And the sudden reappearance of the old playbill convinced her that the show was somehow going to return. And that someone else might die."

Emily leaned forward and butted out her cigarette, exhaling smoke. She looked over at the pack of cigarettes, then up at O. Taking a sip of her tea, she continued her story. She had repeated it time and again in her mind, as one repeats the lines of an unfinished poem, searching for the elusive words that will bring it to an end.

"The initial show took place at the Caledon depot on Saturday, August 8. It was a leap year. Miss Potts discovered that August 8 would again fall on a Saturday that very year, another leap year. She was sure that the show would somehow recur on that day.

"But the depot was no longer in use. My father was busy restoring it that summer with a group of local history buffs. It was to open in the fall as a railway museum.

"As mad as I thought she was, I found myself swept up in her feeling of foreboding. So on August 8, when my father failed to return home before dark from working in the depot, I went looking for him. I pedaled over there on my bike in the pouring rain. As I crossed the threshold of the darkened building, it was as though I had stepped through the door of a dream. The solid world fell away, and I entered the ghostly magic show Miss Potts had described to me in the park.

"I no longer knew who I was or how I had come to be there. The scene flickered like the candles that lit the room. A group of children sat spellbound before a make-shift stage, where a magician was spilling roses from a paper cone. The smell of the roses was overwhelming."

"The smell of roses?" said O, remembering how several times since arriving at the Green Man, she had noticed the same smell.

"Yes," said Emily. "It's like his calling card." And she gave her niece a long probing look.

"The magician saw me standing there and welcomed me to the show. I sat down with the others. The moon was shining in through the open window. Several times, when he asked for a volunteer to assist him onstage, he would fix his gaze on me. It was all I could do not to go, though I could not have said what stopped me. But when it came down to the last illusion, the Decollation of John the Baptist, a memory stirred inside me. When a boy went to walk onto the stage, I stood to stop him and found myself drawn up there in his place. Had it not been for Miss Potts' sudden arrival on the scene to thwart the magician and shatter the spell, he would surely have claimed another victim.

"After it was all over, she made me promise that I would continue to believe in the possibility of the impossible, that I would watch and wait and be ready for him when he came around again.

"I did continue to believe – I became a poet. Every day, poets must believe in the possibility of the impossible. As I guarded the truth of that, so too did I guard the truth of this other, darker thing that had fallen to me."

"Twenty-eight years passed. I spent a lot of it away from home, traveling, working at this and that, living out of a car, with the backseat reserved for the other passenger in my life – poetry. Two suitcases full of pieces of paper salvaged from the storm of life – pieces I would from time to time assemble, like a puzzle without a box, putting out little books and sending them into the world.

"And all the while, in the back of my mind, I could feel the clock ticking away, the months and years slipping by, and the time approaching again when day and date would align as they had then. As that time drew near, I was drawn back here, hoping against hope it was all a madness I had lived through, something that could not possibly happen again.

"I was forty-two when I returned to Caledon. I stayed with your aunt Elizabeth and her family. This was before they up and moved down South. Her daughter, your cousin Alice, had a job that summer at the local library. The new head librarian was planning to stage a Punch and Judy show with an antique set of puppets he'd dis-covered among the large collection housed at the library. He asked Alice if she would assist him in mounting the performance.

"The Caledon depot had been destroyed in a fire years before. I racked my brain, wondering how the magic show could possibly be performed again when the place in which it had occurred was no longer there. The local history material that had been salvaged from the blaze was now being stored at the library. Among the items on display was an old playbill for a magic show.

"Alice had become suspicious of my behavior, so I took her into my confidence. Of course, she thought I was crazy. Nevertheless, as the date grew ever nearer, I became more desperate. Late one night, I came home and found her waiting up for me. She was clearly afraid. She spoke of the change that had come over Mr. Dwyer, the head librarian, since he had begun to work on the Punch and Judy show. It was as if he was under some sort of spell. She suspected it had something to do with the old set of puppets they were using for the show, in particular the frightening devil figure he would play.

"Alice felt a terrible foreboding whenever she was in the library now. And then, that day, something had happened. Out of the blue, Mr. Dwyer informed her he was changing the date of the puppet show. It was to be performed on August 8.

"The blood froze in my veins as I suddenly realized that this puppet show was a manifestation of the same darkness that had informed the magic show Miss Potts and I had seen and that, as the assistant in the show, Alice was in grave danger.

"I knew I had to prevent it from taking place. On the eve of the performance, with her help, I broke into the library. I could feel the magician's presence there, and as I felt my way down the dark stairs into the basement, where the puppets were stored, it was as if I was entering his lair. I found the puppet set and destroyed the devil puppet, with its glowing eyes and its evil grin. And the darker magic was defeated again.

"Afterwards, I decided I'd had enough of moving around, enough of terror. I settled down here in Caledon and put the whole of it out of my mind for a long time. I threw myself into poetry with all my heart. And I threw myself into this shop.

"For years, I absolutely refused to think about it. It was like something that had happened to someone else, in some other lifetime. But all the while, in some dusty corner of myself, I could feel a presence quietly biding its time. It hung about there in the shadows, just out of sight.

"And then a year ago, as the time approached again, it suddenly grew bolder. It would stride out of the shadows and show itself without fear. I tried to frighten it back into hiding, but it stood its ground and mocked me with a grin.

"I began to dream the show again, though it was slightly different now. I saw the magician's face whenever I shut my eyes. I heard his voice whenever silence fell. I don't know how many sleepless nights I must have called your father. I felt that I was going mad, and I'm sure he must have, too.

"Then, one day last fall, I was sitting in the shop and I heard a noise. This shop is haunted by spirits, as I'm sure you know by now. They are friendly spirits, poets largely, most of them not really aware they are dead. But, this day, I looked up and the magician was standing just the other side of the desk, glaring at me. I screamed – and everything went dark. That was when I had my little 'incident,' as they call it. It was Leonard who found me and took me to hospital.

"And now this mysterious playbill has appeared out of nowhere. And I realize that the dreams I have been dreaming these past months are all drawn from it.

"I feel the show approaching again – like a storm on the horizon. The magician is a master of illusion. He can assume any shape he pleases to serve his end. And that end is death. I have no idea what shape he will take this time to lure his victim in. Nor do I have any notion where or how the show will take place. I only know it will come from somewhere I least expect."

26

Things were a little strained between them for several days. O had no idea how to take Emily's story of the magic show. A large part of her wanted to dismiss the whole thing as madness, but another part secretly began counting down the days till August 8.

She tried to make herself busy to avoid the tension that surfaced whenever the two of them were in the same room. She'd planned to paint the outside of the shop and decided this would be the perfect time. Breaking off a piece of the flaking paint from around the front window, she took it to the paint store down the street, matched it with a chip, and bought a gallon of Forest Green. At the same time, she picked up a paint scraper, a large brush, a roller and tray, and a drop sheet.

It was a lovely sunny morning – Saturday, July 25, according to the paper in a newspaper box she passed. She popped the lid off the paint can now, gave the rich thick paint a good stir, and dipped in her brush to begin. A lot of people she knew disliked painting, but O found it calming. It was a chance now to escape the thoughts whirling around in her head.

She decided to hone her skills by starting on the bins for the bargain books. Spreading the drop sheet on the sidewalk under the awning, she set the empty bins on them. She cleaned off the dirt and dust and scraped away the loose paint. Then she applied the first brushstrokes and stood back to admire their deep rich color.

In no time at all, she had finished the first bin and moved on to the second. There was a nice breeze, and the sun was warm on her back. The Green Man swung in the breeze above her, muttering in his creaky, somehow comforting way. She dipped and painted, and her thoughts drifted.

"Hey, that looks really good," said a voice behind her. She turned and saw Rimbaud standing there.

"Thanks," she said, suddenly aware of the shabby clothes she'd pulled on for painting.

"Would you like some help?"

"I'm not sure I could pay you."

"You could always pay me in books," he said with a smile.

"Yeah, I guess I could do that. We've sure got enough of them."

He threw back his head and laughed. "What would you like me to do?" he asked as he took off his jacket and laid it on top of his backpack.

"Well, first we have to prep the wood around the window and on the door before we paint it. What would you say to doing a bit of scraping and sanding?"

"Sounds good."

She got the scraper from the bag of things she'd bought at the paint store.

"Have you used one of these before?"

It would have been a guy thing to claim he had, but he didn't do the guy thing.

"Afraid not," he said with a shrug.

"Well, it's easy. Just run the scraper lightly over the places where the paint is flaking. It works best if you pull it toward you instead of pushing it. Don't press too hard or you'll gouge the wood," she said, demonstrating. "Just light and easy, like this."

"Got it," he said as she handed him the scraper.

"Afterward, we have to sand the scraped areas smooth before we paint."

"You're quite a pro."

"Not really. My dad and I painted the house last year – so I've had a bit of practice." She went back to work on the second bin.

He took a trial scrape on a patch of peeling paint around the window. Flakes rained down onto the drop sheet. "You said you were living here for the summer – staying with your aunt, right?"

"Yeah, my dad's away in Italy, researching a book he's writing on Ezra Pound."

"Ah – Ezra Pound."

"So you know his work?"

"You bet. I love some of the early *Cantos*."

She was impressed.

"He got in trouble for broadcasting anti-American propaganda from Italy for the Fascists during the Second World War, didn't he?"

"That's right," she said. "He was American himself, but he'd spent most of his adult life in Europe. A lot of writers were moving to Europe at the time. He helped promote their work as well writing his own. But he developed some crazy obsessions around politics and monetary reform. That's what led to those radio broadcasts. It was a big mistake.

"When the Allies liberated Italy, they arrested him and put him in a cage in the hot sun for several weeks. If he wasn't crazy before that, he was sure a little crazy afterward. They took him back to the States and tried him for treason. He would probably have been executed, if he hadn't been found insane. He spent the next twelve years in an asylum. Finally, a group of fellow writers managed to get him released."

"You sure know a lot about him."

"Ezra Pound is like a member of the family. My dad's been working on his book about him for years. He went to Italy this summer to visit the city where Pound lived with his daughter after his release and to look at the Pound archives at one of the universities there. He wanted me to come with him, but I've got this thing about planes. Don't ask."

"Is it just the two of you, then? You and your dad?"

"Yeah – oh, and Ezra, of course."

"Do you mind if I ask what happened to your mom?"

"No, I don't mind. She died."

"I'm sorry."

"It's okay. I don't really remember her; I was only two. She was a poet. That's how my dad met her – at a reading. You can't turn around in our family without running into a poet."

"And you?"

"Too soon to say." She tried asking him a few questions about his family, but he deflected them, so she let it go.

They worked while they talked, and the time flew. He knew a ton about poetry. He was easy to talk to as long as she steered clear of personal questions, and it was a break from the tension of being with Emily. The painting went well. He scraped and sanded, and she followed with the paint.

When it was time for lunch, O picked up a couple of croissants at Gigi's.

"Who's the hot guy?" asked Gigi with a wink. "Just point him in this direction when you're done, okay?" She dropped a couple of cookies in the bag. "On the house."

After they'd eaten, O went to fetch the ladder from the back porch to reach the top of the trim around the front window.

"Who's that boy out there with you?" asked Emily.

"It's the guy who came to the reading, the one we got the towel for. He offered to help me paint in return for books. That's okay, isn't it?"

"I suppose so. Does he live around here?"

"I don't know. He says he's new to town."

"Really?" Emily looked past her out the front window, where Rimbaud was busily scraping away the old paint. She didn't say anything more, but from the look on her aunt's face, O was sure she hadn't heard the last of it.

It was ideal painting weather, warm and breezy. By the end of the day, the outside of the shop was transformed. They folded up the drop sheet, swept stray paint flakes from the sidewalk, and taped a WET PAINT sign to the front door and window. It was near closing time.

"Thanks," O said as they stood back to admire it. "You were a great help. It would have taken days to do this without you."

Emily appeared in the front window, pointing to her watch. Her friend Isaac Steiner was supposed to be drop-ping by that evening. O motioned for her to come out and look at the job.

"Very nice," Emily said, giving it the once-over. "It looks like a new place." She cast her eye on the boy.

"Oh – this is Rimbaud," said O.

Emily arched an eyebrow. "Pleased to meet you," she said, but she didn't sound it.

Rimbaud went to shake her hand, then noticed her staring at the paint on it. He drew it back.

"I'd better go and close up," said Emily, heading into the shop.

"I guess I should be going, too," said Rimbaud.

"Would you like to wash your hands first?"

"No, I'll be fine."

"We'll settle up your payment next time you're in the shop," said O.

"No problem. And if there's anything else I can help you with, just let me know."

"Actually, I was thinking I might want to spruce up the sign a little next week. How does Monday sound?"

"Just fine." He slid his jacket back on and shouldered his backpack.

They said a brief good-bye, and he loped off down the street. As O gathered up the paint supplies, she glanced down the street after him, but he had already disappeared.

Since she had carried them upstairs on the day of the poetry reading, the carriage-house books had been sitting on the floor by the couch. They had brought their smell of mildew and damp into the room with them.

It was as if Lawrence Linton himself had entered not only their lives but their living room. O imagined him sitting on the corner of the couch, his glasses dim with dust, a wisp of cobweb strung in his hair, wearing the musty odor of corruption as if it were a new cologne.

While Emily went through the boxes and singled out several items for her friend to look at, O did her best to bring some semblance of order to the flat. She tidied the omnipresent piles of books, rounded up stray articles of clothing, vacuumed cat hair off the couch, dusted the tabletops, and cleared away old cups and plates. By seven o'clock, when the doorbell rang, the place was looking much better.

"I'll get it," she called down the hall, where Emily was closeted in her room, getting ready. She hoped Isaac Steiner would receive a warmer welcome than Rimbaud had. Emily had been positively chilly toward him.

When she opened the door, O found herself face-to-face with a striking older gentleman with a neatly trimmed white beard and bright piercing eyes. A fedora, a feather in the hatband, was perched jauntily on his head. He carried a package under his arm.

"Hello. I'm Isaac Steiner," he said, removing his hat. He had an engaging smile and a lofty brow that emanated intelligence. "I take it you are Emily's niece Ophelia. I can see the family resemblance." They shook hands, and she led him into the shop.

"Where is your aunt?" he asked, looking around.

"Upstairs," she said, nodding toward the staircase.

"Tell me," he said in a low voice, "how is she doing? Is she taking her medicine? Has she stopped smoking?"

"Yes, to the first. We're still working on the second."

He laughed lightly and nodded. She led the way as they negotiated the narrow staircase to the second floor.

Emily was sitting in the living room as they entered. She was wearing a dress O hadn't seen before. With her hair pinned up and a silk scarf tied around her neck, she looked very elegant. She rose and gave Isaac one of her rare embraces.

"How good to see you," she said. "Thank you for coming."

"My pleasure, my dear." He put his hat on the arm of a chair and sat down on the couch beside her. "How has your muse been treating you?"

"My muse is as fickle as always. Weeks go by when she forgets where I live."

"One learns to bear such things," he said. "You're looking well."

"You always were a bad liar, Isaac, but *you* are looking well. Age has been kind to you."

"Well, I'm content."

"And that is the most effective medicine of all. Can I get you a drink?"

"That would be very nice. Actually, I brought along a nice bottle of brandy, if you'd like to open that." He handed her the package. "And then you must show me your find."

"O, perhaps you could lift that pile of books by the couch onto the coffee table for Dr. Steiner, while I go and open this." And she was off.

"Please – not 'Dr. Steiner.' 'Isaac' will do just fine," he said when she had gone. "And you go by 'O,' I gather, rather than 'Ophelia'?"

"That's right." As she leaned down to put the books on the coffee table, the little silver pendant her father had given her popped free of her shirt. His eye went to it immediately.

"I'm sorry to stare," he said. "May I ask where you got the pendant you're wearing?"

"This? Oh, it was a gift from my father," said O as she sat down in her chair.

"I see. And did he tell you what it is?"

"No, only that it's a good luck charm. It has writing on it."

"Yes, I know," he said.

Emily returned with the opened bottle of brandy and three small glasses on a tray. She filled the glasses and passed them around.

"May I propose a toast?" said Isaac, raising his glass. "To health, happiness, and long life."

"Amen to that," said Emily, and they all drank.

O had never had brandy before. She took a big sip and felt the sweet liquid burning her throat.

Isaac began to look through the texts Emily had set aside for him. He seemed quite excited.

"These look mostly like texts of the Lurianic School of Cabala. Luria was the last, and perhaps the greatest, of the cabalists. The books are about the struggle of good and evil in the world . . . the withdrawal of the divine light and the attempt to achieve regeneration through mystical practice. They are extremely rare. It's a shame they haven't been treated better. Where did you say you got them?"

Emily told him about Lenora Linton and her great-grandfather's collection. From there, they got to talking about the mystery of Lawrence Linton's final years.

"It seems to me there was something about a fire," said Isaac. "I believe someone died in it. After that, Linton withdrew from the world. He lived his final years as a recluse."

"That rings a bell," said Emily. "In any event, this is part of his collection."

"The struggle of good against the forces of evil in the world," mused Isaac. "Maybe this was what he was studying in his last years. I wonder what led him down that road. I'll see what I can find out for you, if you'd like."

"That would be wonderful. Perhaps you could take a look at this, too? I believe it's Linton's journal."

He took the book from her and leafed through it. "It's a journal, all right. Curious that he should write it in Hebrew. I'll take it with me and give it a closer look."

They chatted for a while, and then he rose to go.

"I'll get back to you about these books. If something can be done about the moisture damage, I'm sure I could find a good home for them." He gave Emily an embrace. "Thank you for calling me, Emily. It was good to see you again."

"The pleasure was all mine. O, would you see Dr. Steiner out?"

O walked him downstairs. As they stood at the front door, he said, "That pendant you're wearing is called a *kamea*. At one time, they were quite common among Jews. I remember my mother wearing one when I was young. Now people regard them as relics of a more superstitious age. May I see yours?"

She took it off and handed it to him. He turned it over and studied the inscriptions closely.

"These are passages from Scripture. The names of God and several guardian spirits are invoked. This is a very powerful charm, intended to ward off the forces of evil. We seem to have come upon something of a theme – your charm, Linton's books. If I didn't know better, I'd say some evil was abroad." He handed the pendant back to her, and she slipped it on again.

"Good night, O. Take good care of your aunt."

"I will."

"And be careful. The signs seem to be converging here for some reason. And I'm not above a little healthy superstition."

27

"You're sure you're holding on tight?"

"I'm holding on tight."

"And you won't let go?"

"I won't let go."

"Promise?"

"Promise. Look, if you're nervous, why don't you come down, and I'll go up and do it?"

"No, it's okay. I'm fine."

O gripped the ladder with sweaty hands and glanced down to make sure Rimbaud really *was* holding on. She was just five rungs up, but already the backs of her knees felt wobbly and weak, and the ground had that faraway look to it. Suddenly, painting the Green Man sign didn't seem like such a good idea.

You can *do* this, she told herself. It's not really that high. You scoot up and down the ladder in the shop a dozen times a day. But her self wasn't buying it. Her self wanted nothing more than to scurry back down the rickety stepladder and abandon the whole idea. But she couldn't embarrass herself like that – not in front of him.

She coaxed her feet up one more rung. Pushing the paint scraper down securely into her back pocket, she glanced up. If she stood on the second rung from the top, she should be able to reach the sign.

The ladder shook a little, and she let out a scream. Not a big scream, but still a scream.

"Sorry," he called up.

"Don't . . . do . . . that!"

"Sorry," he said again. "The sidewalk's a little uneven."

She detected a giggle. "Are you laughing? I heard a little laugh at the end there."

"No, I'm not laughing. I swear."

"Well, you'd better not, or if I fall, I'll be sure to fall on your head."

She scrambled up two more steps. There. Well, not quite. Her feet were planted on the second rung from the top all right, but she was bent over double, her hands fused to the small wooden platform at the top of the ladder.

People who work heights for a living say you should never look down. In the position she was in now, she had no choice. The sidewalk looked about a hundred feet away, though it was probably no more than ten. Her fear seeped through the soles of her shoes, and the ladder began to tremble. She said a silent prayer, then let go of the ladder and stood up straight. Grabbing hold of the sign, she held on for dear life.

Suddenly she found herself face-to-face with the Green Man. He seemed as surprised to see her up close as she was him. He made that little creaky noise in the back of his throat that he made when he swayed in the wind. It was his way of talking, and she imagined she could do no better herself with two great stalks of vines growing from her mouth.

They had spent so long studying one another from a distance that she felt they were already acquainted. She had long since gone from trying to puzzle out his creaks and groans to imagining what he might be saying.

When she'd first caught sight of him, suitcase in hand, that early morning two months back, he had struck her as grotesque and frightening. Later, the vines that grew from his mouth seemed like some horrible punishment he had been condemned to bear, and her fear had turned to pity. But the longer she was near him, the more he became the guardian presence Emily felt him to be. And there was a strange nobility about him.

Now, face-to-face, she saw more. Features that had been indistinct from the ground were suddenly sharp and clear. What looked like worry from a distance proved up close to be concentration. What seemed a grimace from the ground became up close almost a smile. And suddenly she realized the vines that grew from his mouth, far from being a punishment, were a sort of blessing he bore. For what he bore was life – and in that there was joy.

Tucked in among the leaves of the vines that encircled his head were two small carved birds. All her fear had vanished. She felt as secure on her high perch as the birds that sheltered in the branches. When she looked into the Green Man's eyes, he looked back. The sign gently swayed. And she swayed with it.

He had always seemed ancient to her, his face fissured with wrinkles. But now she saw that the wrinkles were only cracks from the weathering of the wood. Face-to-face like this, he looked ageless.

O stood transfixed. Suddenly, it seemed to her that something sparked deep in his eyes – a flame. She looked deeper, and the flame flared into a fire. She saw dense smoke and, in the midst of the smoke, two figures entwined in one another's arms.

The vision faded, and she found herself perched on top of the ladder again. The sign creaked as it swayed back and forth, and a word sounded clearly from the Green Man's mouth. "Be-ware," said the voice. "Be-ware."

She sprang back in shock, letting go of the sign. For a moment she teetered, trying to gain her balance. Then, suddenly, she was falling. But as the ground rushed up to meet her, her fall was broken.

Rimbaud had caught her. "Are you all right?" he asked as he cradled her in his arms.

"I think so. I lost my balance." She looked into those dark fathomless eyes, and she had the feeling he was about to kiss her.

There was a sudden sharp rap on the window of the shop. She jerked back, and Rimbaud set her down on her feet. Emily was standing in the window with an armful of books, staring at them. Without a word, she turned and disappeared into the shadows of the shop.

O stood in the poetry section, looking at the book Rimbaud had brought back earlier that day. It was the last of the "borrowed" books – a volume of poems by his namesake, Arthur Rimbaud. A photo of the boy poet was on the cover. He bore a striking resemblance to her Rimbaud – something in the eyes, the set of the mouth; something in the regal way he held his head, the deliberately disheveled look of his hair. As she studied the grainy old photo, the memory of her fall from the ladder two days before flooded back.

She opened the book and flipped through it, hoping against hope another poem might fall out. There was no poem, but something else fluttered to the floor – an odd fan-shaped leaf, still green and pliant, as though it had just been plucked. It wasn't the first time she'd found a leaf in one of the books he returned. He used leaves to mark his place.

She brought it to her nose. It had a pungent smell. It was certainly no leaf she recognized. There was nothing remarkably odd about it being there, she supposed. People marked their places in books with all sorts of strange things. But as she held the leaf in her hand and thought of the boy who'd put it there, she sensed it was the hall-mark of some mystery at the heart of him.

With Rimbaud becoming more of a presence around the shop recently, Emily's anxiety level had risen dramati-cally. Last night, she'd taken O aside.

"Listen, O. When your father sent you to stay here, I know he had ulterior motives. He was looking out for me. I appreciate that – and I appreciate everything you've done. You've taken very good care of me – even when I didn't want you to. And you've transformed this place.

"But he also expected me to look out for you. I'm inexperienced at watching over teenage girls, but I was once one myself. I know you like this boy, O. But think about it. What do you know about him? You don't know his real name. You don't know where he comes from. You don't know where he lives. He makes me nervous. I want you to be careful. Very careful."

It was pure craziness, of course, but Emily was so

unremittingly intense about it that it got O going as well. Finding the leaf in the book had decided it. The next time she saw Rimbaud, she was determined to follow him to find out where he lived.

28

O n the last day of July, Emily asked O if she would
mind changing the window display. She normally put up a new display at the beginning of
each month and took it down at the end. Any longer than
that, and the sunlight began to bleach the dust jackets of
the books.

While Emily gathered together the items she had set
aside for the next display, O climbed into the window
area to take down the current one. It had been a sunny
month, and she noticed that some of the dust jackets
had already begun to fade. Each book was accompanied by a handwritten card on which Emily had noted
the price, along with any interesting information about
the book. O removed the cards as she piled the books in
front of her.

The window area was in need of a good cleaning. The
green felt was dingy with age and covered in dust. The
brittle corpses of flies and wasps lay scattered over it.
She decided this would be an ideal time to clean up the

area. She fetched the whisk and dustpan from the back of the shop and, crawling on hands and knees in the narrow space, started sweeping up the dust and dead insects.

In the midst of it, she happened to glance out the window and saw Rimbaud standing outside the fruit and vegetable store across the street. He stood there a long time, and she was afraid he was about to take something. But, instead, he picked up one of the cellophane pack-ages of discounted fruit they'd put there and went into the store. He came out carrying a bag and began walking in the direction he always took whenever he left the bookshop. On the spur of the moment, O decided to follow him.

Clambering out of the window, she called to Emily: "I'm thinking of changing the felt in the window. I'm just going to see if I can find anything. I'll be back in a bit." Without waiting for a reply, she darted out the door.

Rimbaud was already out of sight by the time she hit the street. She walked four blocks with no sign of him. She was about to give up and go looking for a fabric store, when she spotted the familiar lean, loping figure two blocks ahead, on the opposite side of the street. Breaking into a trot, she narrowed the distance between them to a block. She shadowed along behind him, ready to duck into a shop doorway if he should happen to look back.

She had trailed him for twenty minutes, when he suddenly turned off the main drag, crossed a set of tracks,
and entered a sketchy neighborhood she would normally never have ventured into. People hanging out on
the porch steps of the low-rise apartments that lined the
street eyed her as she went by.

Now that there were fewer people around, it was harder
to keep hidden. She hung back farther than she wanted,
afraid of being spotted. She had totally lost her bearings
and wasn't sure how she would find her way home. The
street dipped and rose like a rollercoaster. In no time at
all, she lost sight of him as he disappeared over the crest
of a hill. She broke into a trot, but as she came to the top
of the hill, there was no trace of him up ahead. It was as
if the ground had opened under him.

To her right, a short side street of modest bungalows
shaded by tall maples ended abruptly before a low white
fence with a DEAD END sign posted on it. She turned down
the street, taking in the houses that lined it on either
side. He might have gone into any one of them, but she
didn't think so. She felt sure he'd gone over the fence.

As she approached it, she saw that, on the other side,
the ground fell away into a deep ravine. She scrambled
over the fence and along a crude path tramped through
the weeds, leading to the rim of the ravine. From there,
it launched down the steep hillside and disappeared

from view. The hillside was thick with bushes, saplings, and stunted trees. The floor of the ravine was invisible through the dense canopy of trees that rose to almost street level.

She peered down into the green shadows, looking for signs of movement. All was still. It seemed to her the stillness of something holding its breath, and she was suddenly afraid. She sensed she had come to the world's end. Beyond lay an uncharted realm.

Grabbing on to branches to slow herself, she took a few tentative steps down the hill. The green canopy closed over her like a lid. In the sudden silence, she could hear the hammering of her heart.

Now that she was below the canopy, she could see all the way down to the dappled floor of the ravine, where a path ran alongside a stream. She had no experience of such a wilderness at the very heart of a city. Nothing like this existed in the flat country she called home.

She ventured a little farther down, but her feet kept sliding out from under her, as if the hill were made of glass. It was only by making desperate stabs for branches that she was able to stop herself from hurtling down to the bottom.

Her legs were scratched, and the light flats she was wearing were full of dirt. She wasn't dressed for this. Besides, Emily would be wondering where she was. She decided to head back. The ravine could wait for another day, when she was better prepared to meet it.

It was more difficult getting up the hillside than going down. She wedged her feet at the base of saplings to gain footing on the slick ground. By the time she reached the top, she was panting. Brushing herself off, she climbed back over the fence. A little girl, her face pressed to the window of the last house on the street, looked at her as if she were some creature spawned in the shadows below.

When she got to the head of the street, she glanced back at the white fence and the diamond-shaped DEAD END sign. She hurried home, feeling that she had narrowly escaped some great danger.

Emily was in the back room of the shop when she returned.

"Where on earth have you been, Ophelia?" The dreaded name. "Running off like that with hardly a word. I was worried sick."

"I'm sorry. It was a spur-of-the-moment thing. I thought we could freshen up the front window with a new piece of material, so I went to look for some while the window was empty."

Fortunately, on the way home she had come across a fabric shop and found a suitable piece of green felt. She took it out of the bag to show Emily.

Emily glanced at it, but you could tell she wasn't buying

the story. O could feel her aunt's shrewd eyes taking in the scratches on her legs, the state of her shoes, the something in her eyes that even the walk home had not erased.

She reached out and took a lock of O's hair in her hand. With a quick tug, she pulled something away and held it in the palm of her hand for O to see. It was a burr. O had picked several of the stubborn things off her clothes on the way home, but hadn't noticed the one in her hair.

"It must have been quite a shop," said her aunt.

29

It was a quiet neighborhood. The road meandered through it as if it had all the time in the world. Emily took the same path she always did. She knew the neighbors by name and greeted each one with a quiet nod as she walked by – Louise Labranche, Octavia Talbot, Wallace Root. The houses were small but ample enough for their narrow needs.

Here, someone had planted a little garden; there, another had set a picket fence to mark the bounds of their scant estate. Someone had called on Annie Wray and left a small bouquet of roses at her door, wound with a twist of foil.

The wind tousled the leaves on the trees that arched over the path. The shade trembled, as if the ground beneath her were not as solid as it seemed.

The groundskeepers came and went in their motorized carts, with mowers, rakes, and slack coils of hose, like sleepy green snakes, loaded in back. They fanned out over the grounds and were soon busy cutting and watering the grass. The occasional car crept by.

Emily found her favorite bench, tucked against the trunk of a tall pine. She took her cigarettes from her purse, lit one, and took a long drag. So it had come to this – sneaking cigarettes on the sly. Ah, well. She removed her hat and set it down on the bench beside her. How wonderful the feel of the breeze against her skin, the scent of blossoms in the air, the play of sun and shade on the emerald grass. . . .

"Ah, here you are," said a voice behind her, and a hand alighted on her shoulder. It was Miss Potts.

"I was hoping you might be here," said Emily.

"I'm rarely anywhere else these days," said Miss Potts as she sat down beside her. She looked very prim in her dark flowered dress, with a little lace at the cuffs and collar, her silver hair drawn back into a bun.

Emily noted with quiet concern that her friend's shoes were caked with mud and the laces had snapped in several places.

"I've brought you these," she said, taking a bouquet of daisies from her bag and handing them to her. She also took out a pair of scissors she'd brought from her sewing basket and set them on the bench beside her.

"Lovely," said Miss Potts, admiring the flowers. "Are they from your garden?"

"No, I'm afraid I've let my garden lapse. I haven't felt quite up to it since – oh, never mind."

"No, do tell me."

"It's nothing, really. A mild heart problem. One expects such things at my age." It was too sobering a thought for such a pleasant day. Emily tucked it quietly away. "Shall I get some water for those?" she asked.

"Oh, yes. Would you, my dear?"

A little brass vase was set in a hollow in the ground close by the bench. She pulled it out, put the flowers in, and filled it at a nearby spigot. She took the scissors and tidied up the grass a little, and then put them back in the bag as she sat down.

"There. That's got things looking a little more Protestant, as my dear grandmother used to say." A runner panted by along the path, raising a hand in greeting. "Ah, to be young again," said Emily.

"Yes, indeed," mused Miss Potts.

"My niece has come to stay with me for the summer."

"How nice." Miss Potts reached up and pulled away a blade of dead grass that had caught in the hinge of her glasses.

"Yes, but I fear for her."

"Oh? Why?"

"Because this is the year it's due to come round again."

"I see. And have you told her?"

"Yes, everything. She thinks I'm mad, of course. How could she think otherwise? I am."

"Nonsense. You are a poet – a very good poet. You see more than most."

"I'm afraid for her. I shouldn't have allowed her to come. It was foolhardy. After the last time, I deliberately destroyed everything that had any connection with the show. I hoped that might end it."

"There is no end. You must know that. It will come around again at the appointed time. Have you been dreaming it? That's a sure sign."

"Yes, but it's different this time. *He* is the same, but the show is different. She found a playbill in the shop," she said, reaching into her purse to take it out. She had worried the old thing into tatters. Unfolding it, she showed it to Miss Potts. "I've dreamt the entire show as it's laid out there, all except the last three illusions. What can it mean?"

"I don't know."

"And there's something else. A strange boy has appeared from out of nowhere. She has befriended him."

"You know the magician can assume any shape he chooses."

"I know."

"And he has taken the shape of a boy before."

"I know, but what should I do?"

"The only thing you can do, my dear: watch and wait – and be ready."

"I'm not as strong as I once was. I'm not sure I'm equal to this."

"Have faith. Strength will come from somewhere you least expect."

"I hope you're right."

They sat together quietly for a time. Then Emily gathered up her belongings and put them in her bag. "I should be going now," she said.

But when she turned to say good-bye, Miss Potts was gone.

Delicate plumes of water fanned back and forth across the grass as she made her way back along the cemetery path. Near the front gates, she passed the Linton memorial, a large granite obelisk with the family name carved on its side and, below, the list of the Linton dead.

Had she paused to look, she would have noticed a new name added to the list, the letters cut sharp and clean in the stone, still untouched by weather and time.

O grabbed a corner of the felt and gave it a yank. Several of the tacks holding it in place popped free. One pinged off the window, narrowly missing her head. A cloud of dust rose from the old material and filled the confined space. She gave another yank – more flying tacks, more dust. This time the material tore, and she suddenly remembered what Emily had said about the fabric of time tearing in places, allowing things to pass through.

By the time she'd pulled up all the material, she was coughing like a maniac. She bundled it up, careful to avoid the bristling tacks, then climbed out of the display area and waited for the dust to settle.

She wondered exactly how long the old felt had been in the window. The wood underneath looked ancient. She got a plastic bag from behind the desk and dumped the old material in. Climbing back into the window, she pried up the remaining tacks with a claw hammer and swept the area thoroughly.

She fetched the new fabric she'd bought, a large pair of scissors from the desk drawer, and a staple gun from the battered tool chest on the back porch.

It would have been nice to have another pair of hands to help, but Emily had vanished shortly after breakfast, saying there was someone she had to see. The woman was as high-strung as Psycho, wary of everyone and every-thing. She was constantly looking over her shoulder as if someone was following her.

The condition was contagious. Just being in the shop alone now was making O nervous. The shop ghosts were growing bolder. She kept seeing figures flitting in the shadows, kept hearing furtive little noises in the far room. Switching on the radio, she hoped a good dose of jazz might frighten them off.

She climbed back into the window and unfolded the new piece of fabric. As she draped it loosely over the two shallow tiers that descended to the display area, she was reminded of the steep slope of the ravine where she had followed Rimbaud the other day. It had been a totally crazy thing to do. And what had she gained by it, other than to deepen the mystery surrounding him?

She fit the material roughly in place and trimmed away the excess. She had just started turning the raw edges under and stapling it down, when she had the odd sensation of being watched. She swung around. Rimbaud was standing at the window, staring in.

It might simply have been her imagination, but she couldn't help but feel there was something different in the way he looked at her. She continued feeling it even after he came inside and offered to help lay out the new felt.

They knelt side by side in the display area, tucking and stapling. It went a lot quicker with the two of them working, though it was a tight squeeze in the narrow space. Normally, she would have been happy to be this close to him, but now she felt almost afraid.

"Is there something wrong?" he asked.

"No, nothing."

"You seem awfully quiet."

"Just tired. I didn't sleep well last night. I kept waking up with noises – raccoons or something – on the roof."

They finished tacking down the felt. While she set up the new display, he roamed the store, searching for a book. At that moment, Emily walked through the door. O felt her heart sink. Her aunt would be sure to think it was more than mere coincidence the two of them were together in the shop in her absence. She scrambled out of the window to greet her.

"Well, what do you think?" she asked.

As Emily leaned in to look at the new window area, O glanced over her shoulder, trying to get Rimbaud's attention. He was nowhere in sight.

"It looks great."

"How was your visit?"

"Oh, fine. It's a lovely day. We sat on a bench and chatted." She put down her bag and took off her hat. "I need to talk to you."

"What is it?"

"It's about that boy."

"Emily, maybe we –"

"No, it can't wait. I'm worried. There's something you need to know."

There was a quiet creak of floorboards, and Rimbaud appeared at the far end of the aisle, by the desk. For a long moment, the two stood facing one another. Rimbaud seemed larger, more imposing. He wore a curious expression on his face. The air was charged with tension.

"Did you find anything?" asked O, as cheerfully as she could manage.

"Yeah, this," he said and came to show her the book he had chosen.

"Perfect," she said. "Thanks again for your help with the window."

"My pleasure." With a quick nod in Emily's direction, he was out the door.

O and Emily traded glances. Then Emily picked up her bag and walked back through the shop and upstairs to the flat.

O stood looking out the window. She was glad Emily hadn't seen the book Rimbaud had selected. It was a book on magic.

30

Among the things ranged onstage prior to the magician's performance that night was a long low wicker basket, somewhat the shape of a coffin. During the show, the magician drew many of the props he required from it. The children were amazed at the sheer number of things he took from it, and when they felt it could not possibly contain one more thing, the magician removed yet another object from the basket. It seemed to be a bottomless well from which he could draw whatever he wished.

Finally, however, it appeared he had come to the end of it. For now the magician walked over to the basket and, instead of reaching into it, turned it on its side so that everyone in the room could see it was quite empty.

"How are we to proceed with the show?" he asked. "For it seems our inexhaustible trunk is exhausted. But wait, there is one small item left." The audience strained to see what he saw inside that they could not.

As he reached into it, one or two children noticed a glint of metal catching the candlelight. And, as the magician straightened, they all saw the long curved blade and the jewel-encrusted handle of the sword he held in his hand.

"This sword, my friends, was a gift to me from the sultan of Khadiz. It has been through many battles and tasted much blood, but none who possessed this sword has ever tasted defeat. Now, alas, it is far from the battlefield and waits patiently for the next illusion in tonight's show, when, for a brief time, it will be called back into service – for the illusion entitled the Indian Basket.

"I will require the assistance of a volunteer – some brave, adventurous spirit who is not afraid of darkness or danger. And, of course, for assisting in the show, our volunteer will receive a copy of the professor's little book, which explains the secrets of the magical arts you are witnessing tonight."

A murmur went through the room as neighbor turned to neighbor, each wondering if the other might have the courage to venture up onstage. Finally, a boy sitting by himself near the back of the room stood up. He was tall and thin, and his clothes were too small for him.

There was an awkwardness to his movements as he made his way toward the stage, as if his limbs were wired together like a marionette's. The other children shifted over slightly to let him by, muttering to one another and tittering into their hands, so that the sound of it moved through the room. He kept his eyes fixed on the floor, too shy to meet their gaze, as if he was used to their laughter and had turned inward to shut it out.

As the boy stepped from the shadows into the flickering light of the stage, the magician welcomed him and asked him his name. He muttered something inaudible as his eyes scanned the ground at his feet.

The children laughed louder now, more assured in their mockery, as though the boy had been brought onstage for their amusement. His feet did an unhappy shuffle against the wood of the stage, and his hands clenched and unclenched at his side. It appeared to take every ounce of his courage to stand so exposed before them.

The magician understood it all. "Tell us your name again," he said, "so that even the mouse in the corner over there can hear you." And his hand fell lightly on the boy's shoulder. A shudder went through the boy, and he raised his eyes to look the magician full in the face.

"Carl," he said, with a boldness no one would have expected of him moments before. "My name is Carl." He looked deep into the magician's eyes, cocking his head ever so slightly to the side, as though words were passing between them that no one else in the room could hear.

"Very good," said the magician. "I'm sure even the little mouse in his hole could hear that."

The boy smiled, and with that smile appeared to come a new confidence. The children looking on were stunned into silence. But the boy took no notice of them. His attention was all on the magician's eyes.

"Now, Carl, I would like you to take this sword and examine it carefully. Remember, the blade is very sharp." He held the sword flat in the palms of his hands and passed it to the boy. As the boy took it by the handle, his eyes danced over the jewels, glimmering in the candlelight.

"Now, Carl, this sword possesses great power. It was a sword only the bravest of the sultan's warriors was allowed to touch. It brought invincibility to its bearer in battle."

A smile passed over the boy's face, and he raised the sword.

"Can you feel its power?" asked the magician.

"Yes," said the boy. Everyone in the room could hear him now.

The magician raised his hand in the air, and an apple appeared in it. "Now, Carl, I would like you to pass the sword very lightly over this piece of fruit to demonstrate to our audience just how sharp it is."

The boy ran the blade of the sword across the apple, and it passed through it with the ease of a warm knife through butter. The twin pieces fell to the floor. A murmur ran through the crowd as the upturned halves wobbled to rest and the blade of the sword gleamed in the gaslight.

"Now, Carl," said the magician, taking the sword from the boy, "I want you to step inside this basket here and lie down."

Without the slightest hesitation, the boy lay down inside the long narrow basket, disappearing from view.

"You remember, Carl, that I asked for a volunteer of unusual courage. Are you that one?"

"Yes," came the voice from the basket.

"And you are not afraid of the dark?"

"No," said the voice.

"Very well, then," said the magician, and he closed the lid and secured it with a length of cord. A hush fell over the room.

The magician went over to the table and picked up the sword. He fixed the audience with his eyes. Then, without a word, he walked to the basket and thrust the blade of the sword through it, so that the point pierced the other side.

Several children shrieked in terror as the blade emerged red with blood. Twice more he ran the basket through with the sword. A terrible silence had fallen over the room. All eyes were on the basket, sitting deathly still on the stage.

The magician wiped the blade clean as he contemplated the crowd, then set the sword down on the table. "Life and death," he said as he began to untie the cord that secured the basket. "What are they? Is death no more than a dream from which we soon awake?"

The cord fell slack, and the magician tipped the basket over on its side so that the lid fell open with a dull slap against the floor of the stage.

There was no boy, no blood, only an empty basket that had once been the storehouse for countless props and, for one impossible moment, a site of terror.

"Reality or illusion?" said the magician with a smile. "Which is which?"

There was a faint rustling in the shadows behind the stage, and out into the light strode the boy, as sound and healthy as ever. But he moved now with a new authority. As he took the little book from the magician's hand and made his way offstage, he looked directly into the faces of those who had formerly been his tormentors. They looked back with awe and moved aside to allow him to pass as he returned to his place.

The show continued.

31

In the dream O was at another poetry reading, but this time Rimbaud read. It seemed every word was meant for her alone. She was so overcome with emotion that, when he sat back down beside her, she leaned over and kissed him. But instead of the full warm lips she imagined, those that met hers were as cold and lifeless as glass. She woke from the dream with a sick feeling in the pit of her stomach. It was Saturday, August 8.

Whatever terror it held for her, she knew she had to return to the ravine. Emily had said the magician was a master of disguise. But whatever shape he might assume, O knew one thing for certain: he would not come with fangs and claws. He would have the allure of mystery about him, the fascination of the unknown. He would appear as if from nowhere, without warning and without history, and he would mesmerize with his words. He could be young or old, male or female; for he could change age and sex as easily as one changes a suit of clothes.

Despite everything O's heart told her about Rimbaud, Emily had planted a seed of doubt. Where had he appeared from so suddenly? Where did he live? Why did she have the constant feeling he was with her even when he was nowhere near?

Maybe Emily's madness was not so mad at all. Perhaps, with Rimbaud, she was in the presence of someone not wholly human. Perhaps he had simply stepped into this world for a time, taken this shape to suit his purpose. When he had accomplished that, he would step back again and vanish without a trace. Maybe that was what the line in his poem meant: "In dark of night, I spin this dream of flesh."

She knew he had noticed a change in her. She felt utterly transparent around him, as if he could pick through her thoughts with the same ease that he plucked books from the shelves of the Green Man. Now that she'd decided what she must do, she had to keep her distance from him or he would instantly know her intentions.

After breakfast, she busied herself around the shop. It bothered her to keep Emily in the dark, but she would never have agreed to what O had in mind. Recently, Rimbaud had taken to dropping by in the early afternoon to see if there was anything that needed doing around the shop.

A little after noon, O told Emily she had to go downtown for a while. If Rimbaud came by while she was out, there were boxes on the back porch to be flattened and bundled and a bag of books to be taken down to the Sally Ann. That would keep him busy.

She went up to her room, put on jeans, a long-sleeved tee shirt, and a pair of running shoes, then slipped out the window and down the fire escape. Soon, the shop was far behind her. She followed the route by memory, threading her way through the maze of streets traced indelibly in her mind since the day she followed Rimbaud to the ravine.

Finally, she turned down the silent dead-end street. Climbing the low wooden fence, she tramped through the stand of goldenrod and burdock that bordered the ravine and stood at the edge, looking down into the green dark.

The voice in her head – the reasonable, daylight voice – was doing its best to talk her into turning around and heading straight back home. What did she hope to prove in the end? What did she expect to find? Some sign that Rimbaud was living here? Some proof he was not who he said he was, but a shape the magician had assumed? The whole idea was madness, said the voice. She had strayed too close to Emily's erratic orbit and been pulled in herself, and now she, too, was caught up in this crazy fantasy her aunt had spun.

The sunlight was warm on her face. Behind her stood the quiet houses, secure in their calm. The reasonable part of her was very convincing. Its arguments made perfect sense. She listened to the voice and was tempted to turn back to the world of light.

But then she looked down into the shadows of the ravine. And wound in with the chatter of squirrels, the song of birds, and the rustle of leaves in the wind, she could hear Emily, telling her incredible tale. It was the other side of her that heard that voice – the side that did something so unreasonable as write poems, that peopled the shadows of the Green Man with presences when she was alone in the shop, that lay fearfully in bed and imagined footsteps on the deck in the dark, that dreamt the unimaginable and woke to find it real.

Her heart was pounding in her chest. She said farewell to all the shuttered houses on the shuttered street and started down.

The way seemed less perilous than before. Her runners were not as slick as her flats had been. Roots seemed to hunch up from the ground to give her footholds. Branches bent down for her to latch on to. She passed silently through the green portal and entered the twilight world of the ravine.

Halfway down she heard a voice – a voice composed of furtive scurryings, the distant babble of water, the insistent whispering of the wind in the trees.

Welcome! She felt as if she had entered a room lit by gas-light, and a chalk-white face had leaned out over the skirt of the stage and spoken to her. At a sound of scurrying in the undergrowth, she spun around, expecting a tall stranger dressed in black to be standing there, smiling at her. And the words that spilled from his mouth would branch and leaf and launch themselves up into the low limbs of the trees and curl and wind there, until it seemed the whole of this green world had sprung from his melodious mouth.

A squirrel, darting across the carpet of leaves, raced up the trunk of a tree and chattered down at her. Good Lord, girl, get a grip, she told herself. She breathed slowly, trying to calm herself. The last thing she needed was to panic. Panic and she would be in the power of whatever it was that made its home here.

The steep pitch began to smooth out as she neared the base of the hill. Her eyes adjusted to the dim light, and she moved with ease. She turned and looked back up the hillside, piecing out the path she had taken. She was afraid that if she were to come up in some other place, she would be unable to get out. She knew there was a way out here, so it was here she would go back up. She decided to mark the spot.

The moss-covered trunk of a fallen tree lay half-hidden among spindly saplings and wildflowers by the bank of the stream that ran through the ravine. She stooped to pick up a branch and scraped a crude arrow shape in the damp ground, pointing to the place where she'd come down. She plunged the sharp end of the branch into the soft soil, then moved a few yards off and looked back, wondering if she would see it.

She noticed a plastic bag snagged on a fallen branch, bobbing in the water of the stream. She reached down and freed it, dumped out the slimy water inside, and tied the bag by the handles to the top of her marker. A breeze caught it and it ballooned out from the side of the stick. She was sure to see it now.

She took a quick glance at her watch. It was going on three. The sun sifted down through the canopy of leaves that enclosed the ravine. She would just look around a little and then head back, while there was still plenty of light. The thought of being down here as night fell filled her with terror.

She began walking along the bank of the stream. Her plan was to follow it as far as she could go. She had no idea where it ended, but if she stayed close to the water, she would keep her bearings; and if she wandered off for any reason, she need only find her way back to it and she would know instantly that upstream lay her marker and a safe way out.

Caledon was scored with an intricate network of ravines. Over the years many had been filled in, their streams buried, homes and businesses built over them. But where the ravines were too wide or deep, they were left untouched, remnants of the wilderness that had once covered the land.

Yet, even here, civilization had left its mark. Bits of trash littered the stream and lined the bank. Here, a bicycle frame, rusting in the water; there, a car tire lying among the weeds. A battered shopping cart, a broken chair, bundles of discarded flyers swelling around the plastic ties that held them together – unwanted things that had found their way here.

At one spot, it looked as if someone had backed a pickup to the edge of the ravine and dumped its contents down the hillside – drifts of crumbling drywall, scrap lumber, bags full of garbage. The green world accepted it all without complaint and slowly covered it over.

She didn't know what she was looking for, but she was sure she would know it when she found it. Some sign of him, some habitation hidden among the bushes – something. As she picked her way along the muddy bank, the sound of traffic from the upper world drifted down like a faded memory, and she suddenly remembered her dream on the train.

The stream meandered along the floor of the ravine. She saw the shell of an old stove half-hidden in the under-brush at the base of the hill, a tire swing secured to the branch of a willow bending over the stream. Creatures of the ground and air scattered at her approach. She stepped carefully over slick boulders and fallen branches, scanning the dense green on either side, whirling at the slightest noise, her nerves all on edge.

There were signs of people everywhere, but she felt utterly alone. An hour fled by, and she had found nothing. She was just about to abandon the search and head home – when she turned and saw it.

At first it seemed no more than a darker shadow etched against the shadows, a deeper green against the green. She stopped – and there was a hush all around. She listened – and it was as though every living thing that called this place home listened along.

The thick green canopy closed down on the ravine like a lid on an emerald box, and in the vast silence, she could hear the hammering of her heart.

32

O stood staring at the spot, as the form among the leaves slowly took shape. It stood about five feet high, rising slightly at the center. At first she took it for a crude fort some boys had built among the trees. But as she drew nearer, she saw how skillfully it had been made.

It was as if a spell had been spoken and the supple green saplings that grew everywhere had been charmed to lean into one another, twisting and weaving to form the walls of a green dome. On the side that faced the stream, she noticed a panel of woven branches that must surely be a door.

"Hello," she called. "Is anyone there?"

In this place full of signs of human presence, here was something different. The hillside and the banks of the stream were littered with castoffs. This was no castoff; it was a creation. As she marveled at it, her fear edged aside a little.

She stepped forward, took hold of the door, and shifted it to one side. It teetered a moment, then toppled softly onto the carpet of leaves – the strange fan-shaped leaves Rimbaud used for marking his place in the books he borrowed. She crept closer and stooped to peer inside. Growing bolder, she poked her head through the doorway.

A low table, made from an old cupboard door resting on four paint cans, stood in the center of the hut. Stub ends of candles were stationed at the corners, rooted in pools of hardened wax. On the surface was a box of wooden matches, a plastic water bottle, a pad of pale blue paper, several pencils sharpened by hand, a chipped cup and plate, a clock with a cracked face. Bits of broken glass anchored in wax were ranged around the edge.

She hesitated for a moment in the doorway, then ventured in. It was too low inside to stand, too uncomfortable to stoop. The smooth hump of a log lay along one side. She sat down on it and took in her surroundings.

A knife blade was plunged into a piece of wood by the table, the floor around it littered with shavings. A carved face was worked in the wood – unfinished, still seeking form. From the inner wall of the hut, more carved faces looked down at her. Leaves and branches poked through their open mouths.

Across from her, a piece of mirror was fixed to the wall. Below it, a chipped enamel basin, with a cloth draped over its edge, rested on an upended crate. A bed of leaves and branches was piled on the floor against the wall, a sleeping bag rolled up on it. Something sticking out of the sleeping bag caught her eye. She leaned over, gave a quick tug, and then sprang back as the sleeping bag uncoiled. Lying on it was the book on magic Rimbaud had claimed from the shop.

It was not the book that froze her to the spot, but what lay alongside it, leaving its drift of yellowed flakes on the green fabric of the sleeping bag. Another playbill for the magic show. The sight of it confirmed all she had feared. Staring down at it in disbelief, she backed toward the door.

"What are you doing here?" said a voice behind her.

She whirled around. Rimbaud stood there, framed in the narrow doorway. For an instant, all she saw was the bloodless face of the magician. She barreled into him, knocking him aside, and ran for her life.

She crashed along the bank of the stream, skidding on the soggy ground, her breath coming in ragged gasps. She could hear him close behind, yelling for her to stop. But stopping was the last thing in the world she was about to do. She tore through bushes that had sprouted fingers, stumbled over roots that groped blindly from the muddy ground. Her only thought was to find the marker she had planted by the stream. If she could only reach it and scramble back up the hillside . . .

She never saw what she tripped over. But, suddenly, she was spiraling as if in slow motion through the air. She came down with a splash in the stream, smacking the back of her head on a rock. As she stared vaguely up at the dappled canopy high overhead, she felt herself floating. There was no panic, only a strange sense of irony as she remembered that other Ophelia, falling

> *"in the weeping brook. Her clothes spread wide,*
> *And mermaid-like, a while they bore her up. . . ."*

She saw a familiar face bending over her, a mouth speaking silent words. She felt nothing – nothing but a soft blackness slipping over her, the sunlit canopy gone black, starless, deeper than deepest night.

> *"Til that her garments, heavy with their drink,*
> *Pulled the poor wretch from her melodious lay*
> *To muddy death."*

When she came to, O thought she was lying in the attic room above the Green Man. She opened her eyes, but instead of the low sloping wall that should have been above her bed, she was staring into an intricate weave of vines and branches. She was too dazed to move, too dull for the truth of where she was to register clearly.

A face swam into view – Rimbaud, bending over her, a look of concern on his face.

"How are you? You cracked your head pretty good."

She reached up and felt a bump. She took the measure of the way to the door, the possibility of making a dash for freedom – then realized she was in no shape to dash anywhere.

"Don't hurt me," she said.

"Hurt you? Why in the world would I want to hurt you?"

The way he said it, the way he looked at her, the way his hand came to rest on top of hers made her instantly doubt everything. She tried to sit up. He cupped his hand behind her head to help her.

"You sure you're up to this?"

"Yeah, I'm okay." She felt a little battered, a little damp. He had draped his coat over her. Now he took it and put it around her shoulders. He dunked the cloth in the basin of water, wrung it out, and pressed it gently over the bump. The touch of his hand calmed her. Then her eyes fell on the copy of the playbill on the table by the bed and she grew rigid.

He read her thoughts. "What? This? I found it."

"Where?"

He paused for a moment. "It was stuck to the handrail of the fire escape behind the Green Man."

"The fire escape?" she said incredulously. "Why would it be there? Why would *you* be there?"

He removed the cloth, then turned and sat down on the log, resting his arms on his knees and fixing her with those incredible eyes.

"I was watching out for you."

"When?"

"At night."

She remembered the many times she'd been perched on the edge of sleep and swore she heard light footsteps on the deck outside her room.

"But why?"

"Because it's not safe now." He looked at her intently, and she had the sudden sense that he knew everything.

"We'd better get you back; your aunt will be worrying. Can you manage?"

"I think so." He helped her to her feet and out into the open air. He carefully closed the opening, and the hut melted back into the bush.

On the way through the ravine, she was in a bit of a daze. Her head was whirling, and it was not simply because of the bump. She had clearly been wrong about Rimbaud. But it had done nothing to dispel the mystery surrounding him. That had only deepened.

It was too much to think about now. She followed along

behind him, setting her feet down where his showed the way. When they got to the hill, he took her hand and guided her up the steep grade.

They stood together at the top of the ravine, back in the world of light.

"How are you?" he asked.

"Better," she said. As they walked along the street, her clothes dried in the sun. She kept expecting him to ask her why she'd been poking around in the ravine. But he never did.

Soon they were on familiar ground. It was getting late. She was going to be in deep trouble. The last thing she needed was for Emily to see her with Rimbaud.

"I'm okay from here," she said.

"You sure? You still look a little wobbly to me."

"Really, I'm fine."

"Okay, I'll leave you." He took a few steps, then turned back. "I'm sorry," he said.

"Me, too."

She watched him till he was out of sight. Then she made her way home as fast as she could.

33

While O had been picking her way warily along the banks of the stream in the ravine, Emily was back in the shop, poring over one of the carriage-house books she'd brought downstairs and doing her best to forget what day it was. Still, now and then, a wave of dread would suddenly wash over her, leaving her limp.

When the telephone rang, she nearly jumped out of her skin. She expected it to be O and was ready to give her an earful for having disappeared so long. It had something to do with that boy, she was sure. He'd shown up at the shop around one and, as soon as he learned O wasn't there, had hurried off.

But when she picked up the phone, she was surprised to hear the voice of Lenora Linton.

"Hello," said Miss Linton in her slow, measured manner. "Is this Miss Endicott? It's Lenora Linton calling."

"Hello, Miss Linton. How nice to hear from you. I thought you would have moved by now."

"I've been unavoidably delayed. The buyer for the collection has withdrawn his offer. It seems the financing fell through."

"I'm sorry to hear that." A faint tremor of hope stirred in her breast.

"Forgive me, Miss Endicott, I'm afraid this is rather awkward. But since you had made an offer on the collection already, I was wondering if you might still be interested."

Emily sat bolt upright in her seat. She tried to keep the excitement from her voice. "Yes, I might still have an interest – if the price was right."

"Well, I'm rather up against a wall right now, as you can imagine. I'm sure we could work out something agreeable to both of us. Could you possibly drop by today?"

"Today?" Her mind was racing a mile a minute. "Couldn't it wait until tomorrow?"

"I'm afraid I really must leave tonight."

"I see, but I'm alone in the shop right now. And I'd have to contact my bank, of course. I'm not sure I could get everything in order that quickly."

"I understand perfectly. Forgive me for troubling you, Miss Endicott. I thought it might be worth a try. Goodbye." And with a quiet click, the line went dead.

Emily sat at the desk in a state of shock. Her hands would not stop shaking. The find of a lifetime had slipped through her fingers not once, but twice. It was more than she could bear. Quickly gathering her thoughts, she decided to close the shop early and leave a note for O. She called the bank to confirm that the line of credit she had set up earlier was still in place, then rifled through her Rolodex for the Linton number.

She dialed with trembling fingers. The line was busy. Miss Linton was no doubt talking to someone else about the collection. She hung up, waited a few minutes, and called again. Miss Linton answered on the second ring.

"Hello?"

"Miss Linton, it's Emily Endicott. I've been able to make the necessary arrangements. I could come by today, and we could talk."

"That would be splendid."

She glanced up at the clock, estimating how long it would take to pull herself together, close the shop, and get over to the Linton house. "Shall we say five o'clock?"

"Five would be fine. I look forward to seeing you."

Emily had been so preoccupied when she woke up that morning that she had pulled on the first things that came to hand. She changed into something more presentable now and ran a brush through her hair, while staring into the startled eyes of the old woman in the mirror.

Putting her checkbook in her purse, she went downstairs

and switched off the lights in the shop. She turned the sign in the window to CLOSED and locked the door behind her. On her way to the car, she realized she had forgotten to leave the note for O. There wasn't time to go back now. She would try to call while she was out.

The car started on the first try; she took it to be a good sign. As she threaded her way through the sunlit streets, a breeze blew cool upon her face, and she felt the cloud that had settled over her these past few weeks begin to lift. A new optimism flowed through her and, with it, the conviction that things were about to turn her way.

She found the little cul-de-sac street without even thinking about it, as though the car had driven there by itself. Parking around the corner, she walked to the house. The house next door was no more. Even the rubble had been cleared, leaving a flat empty lot with a startling view of the ravine beyond.

There was a hollow sound when she knocked. She heard approaching footsteps. Miss Linton opened the door, looking wan and frazzled. She had a kerchief tied in her hair. "Miss Endicott, do come in. I'm afraid the place is in rather a state. I'm arranging some last minute things for the movers to pick up tomorrow, after I've gone."

The hall was a jumble of boxes. The pictures had been taken down, and the rug had been rolled. Their footsteps echoed on the bare wooden floor.

"I'll just show you to the library," said Miss Linton. "I imagine you'd like to have another quick look at the collection."

Emily followed her up the stairs and along the hall, glancing through open doors at empty rooms shrouded in shadows. Miss Linton walked her as far as the foot of the narrow staircase that led to the turret room.

"The room felt damp. I laid a fire for you. There's tea on the table. Please help yourself. I'll be back shortly, and we'll talk business." She hurried off down the hall, muttering fretfully to herself.

Emily mounted the stairs and entered the library. The fire burned pleasantly in the grate. A silver tea service sat on the table. The books were ranged on the surrounding shelves. She felt like a child in a toyshop.

She'd brought along her notes on several titles she had researched following her first look at the collection. She took those books down now and went through them, confirming the details. It was a marvelous collection! She could hardly believe it would soon be hers.

It would fetch a very good price. The titles in the magic section were extremely rare. She scanned the books on the shelves again – histories of stage magic and magicians, early volumes linking magic with witchcraft – one rarity after another. The profit she stood to make from the sale of these alone would more than cover her costs.

Time passed. She wondered what was keeping Miss Linton. No doubt she had much to do. No point in putting up a fuss. Emily still hoped she could finesse the price a little. Pouring herself a cup of tea, she surveyed her estate. There was that sound of cooing she had heard last time. In a minute, it passed.

Miss Linton had left a few empty boxes on the floor of the room. Emily presumed they were for her. She began carefully boxing a few of the prize items she hoped to carry away with her today. As for the rest, she would arrange for Miles to accompany her, sometime over the next couple of days, to pick them up. A smile came to her face as she imagined his reaction to this find they had dreamt of for years.

Here was something she hadn't seen before – a thin booklet in paper wraps entitled *Secrets of the Magic Art*. She looked in vain for a date. It was cheaply produced, the printing uneven, and the binding no more than a simple stitch. Nonetheless, it was a curious little volume and, no doubt, quite rare.

She sat down with it in the comfortable chair before the fire. It carried her off as soon as she started to read. There was something arresting in the tone of the writing. For all its crudeness, there was a note of solemnity to it, a sense that magic in whatever guise was something not to be taken lightly. It cautioned devotees of the art to enter into its study with heart and mind prepared. Following the introduction, a number of magical feats were described – with no suggestion that they were illusions, but rather an underlying presumption that magic was a real and potent power.

The fire crackled in the grate. She found herself glancing up at it from the pages of the book. It was hypnotic. She took another sip of the tea. Her eyes felt heavy. Her mind was playing tricks with her. As she stared into the fire, she saw faces in the flames, heard voices in the crackling of the wood.

In some dim corner of consciousness, Emily knew she ought to be getting home. But with the book and the tea and the heat of the fire, all that began to fade. A lethargy crept over her and, with it, a feeling of absolute peace. She felt as she had on those long lazy summer afternoons in the sun when she was young.

It was as if some high forbidding wall she had been standing in front of had suddenly fallen away. A wondrous sense of endless possibilities stretched out before her. Lines of poetry floated fully formed into her mind. There was magic in the air, and she fell willingly into its warm embrace.

She closed her eyes and laid her head back against the chair. A delicious lassitude spread like sweet warm light through all her limbs. And she slept.

The old woman who had entered the room lay slumped in the chair like a castoff coat, and a young woman full of life and light rose and walked through her dreams.

The book slipped from her hands and fell quietly to the floor.

34

O looked through the window at the restaurant clock. It was almost six o'clock. She was going to be in serious trouble. That worried her a lot more than the bump on the back of her head and the dull ache that went with it. She tried to concoct a plausible-sounding story as she hurried along the street, knowing full well Emily would instantly see through it and suspect she had been with Rimbaud.

As she came in sight of the shop, something struck her as odd. The sign in the window had been flipped to CLOSED, but the blind hadn't been pulled and the bargain bins hadn't been taken in. The weekend paper, which normally came before four, was wedged in the mail slot.

Emily must have closed the shop early – and hurriedly. O had left shortly after noon. Rimbaud must have come by a little later. When he discovered she wasn't there, he would have left and made his way back to the ravine. The sight of them both taking off would have set Emily's antennae quivering. She was strange, but she was no fool.

Could she possibly have followed Rimbaud? Somehow O couldn't picture her aunt slinking along the streets after him. But where was she, then?

O hadn't bothered to take her keys with her when she left the shop. She banged on the door now and rang the upstairs bell, hoping Emily was up in the flat. But why had she closed in such a hurry? Had she been taken ill? Had all the stress surrounding this day triggered another attack?

Her stomach knotted into a tight ball. She stood back and looked up at the blank upper windows, then pounded on the door so loudly that a couple passing on the other side of the street stopped to stare.

Suddenly, she had an idea. Dashing down the side of the building, she flung open the back gate and took the fire escape stairs two at a time. As she came up onto the deck, she saw Psycho sunning herself on one of the dingy plastic chairs. The cat had come out through the window O was praying she'd inadvertently left open. They both made a mad dash for it now.

She flung the window wide and clambered in. "Emily!" she cried as she raced through her room and down the flight of stairs to the kitchen. "Emily!" She hurried through the living room, then down the hall to her aunt's bedroom. The clothes Emily had been wearing earlier were draped over a chair, and her hat and handbag were gone from the hook on the closet door. Her workroom was locked from the outside.

O hurried back along the hall. She opened the door leading to the shop and started down the stairs, hoping to find some clue as to where Emily had disappeared. Psycho sped down before her.

Mallarmé sat hunched on the stairs, his plaid shawl draped over his shoulders, his pen poised over a scrap of closely written manuscript on his knees. She sidestepped him on her way down. He glanced up briefly, as if he had felt a ghost walk over his grave.

Ghosts had claimed the empty shop. Timid Miss Dickinson flitted out of sight as O appeared. In the back room, Pound was slumped on the couch, his legs crossed, his hand running over his furrowed brow, deep in thought. A Chinese text lay open on his lap. With his free hand he stroked Psycho, who had jumped up on the couch beside him and studied O warily as she stood in the doorway.

Borges, the blind Argentinean poet who had recently become a presence in the shop, was up the ladder in the front room, looking for something. His face was pressed close to the spines of the books, for his eyesight, though restored in death, was dim.

O let them be. They had become part of the place – like the lizards that crawl on the walls in tropical climes. If you didn't mind them, they didn't mind you.

She maneuvered through the narrow gap in the bunker of books that was the desk at the Green Man. The Rolodex was sitting by the phone, opened to Lenora Linton's name. But why? Lenora Linton was supposed to have moved by now. Could Emily possibly have gone to the Linton house?

As she walked back up the stairs to the flat, the phone rang. She hurried to the living room to get it, hoping it might be Emily. It was Isaac Steiner.

"Is your aunt home, O?" he asked.

"No, I'm afraid she's out at the moment."

"I wonder if you could give her a message for me? It's about Lenora Linton. I told her I'd see what I could find out about her. Now, this is rather curious. It seems that Lenora Linton died a little over a year ago."

"What?"

"So whoever your aunt has been doing business with, it certainly isn't Lenora Linton. . . . Hello? Hello?"

But O had dropped the receiver and was making a mad dash for the door.

It took Emily a moment to realize where she was when she woke up. The fire had died down to a few pale flames amid the glowing ghosts of logs, and the room had filled with shadows. She glanced at her watch and saw that it was getting on to eight o'clock. She ought to have been home long ago. O would be wondering where she was. She began to gather up her things.

Her eye fell on the books she had spread over the table. The sight of them filled her with longing. What could have happened to Miss Linton? She noticed that the little book she had been reading before she fell asleep had fallen to the floor.

She picked it up and thumbed through it once again. It had a strange allure. It would take nothing for her to slip it into her handbag. Miss Linton would never notice its absence and, besides, it would soon be hers.

She pushed the thought from her mind but, as she picked up her handbag, she found herself unaccountably releasing the clasp and reaching for the little gem. No sooner was it in her hand than she heard a noise at the door.

She dropped the book as if it had caught fire, and the thought passed through her mind that she had somehow been observed. Simultaneously, the handle of the door turned, and a wedge of light lit the wall as it opened. Into the room came Lenora Linton, carrying a candle in a pewter holder.

"Forgive me, Miss Endicott, you must have thought I'd forgotten you. There are so many things to be settled before I leave tonight. My mind is all awhirl. And now it appears the power has been turned off. We'll muddle through somehow."

She went to the table and put down the candle. With a regal sweep of her hand, she motioned Emily to a chair. "Do sit down," she said and breathed a deep sigh as she settled herself. "Ah, that's better. This is far too much running about for an old bird like me."

Looking at the dying fire, she ambled over to give it a poke. The embers settled, and flames sprang up with a *whoosh*.

"I presume you've had an opportunity to examine the collection again."

"Yes," said Emily. It seemed that the older woman was looking pointedly at her handbag.

"And is everything in order?"

"Perfectly."

"Fine. Then perhaps we can attend to the business at hand."

"Of course." Emily reached for her handbag, opened it – and froze. For tucked in among her things was the little book. But how?

"Is something wrong, Miss Endicott?"

"No, nothing at all. I just realized, I . . . I forgot to bring a pen." As she rummaged through the bag for her checkbook, she was careful to hold it close, so that Miss Linton could not see in.

"No, here it is, after all." She took the checkbook and pen from the bag and closed it carefully.

Miss Linton fixed her with an intense look, her lips curling slightly in the hint of a smile. Emily felt as tremulous as the flame that danced atop the candle. She opened the checkbook and uncapped the pen.

"Shall I make it out to you?" she asked.

"That would be fine."

"And the amount?"

"Shall we say five percent off the figure we discussed earlier – for the inconvenience I've caused you?"

"That's most generous." She was aware of Miss Linton leaning forward in her chair to watch her as she wrote out the check and signed her name. From somewhere in the depths of the house came a scurrying sound. She looked up at Miss Linton, her face pale in the candlelight.

"You've forgotten something," said the older woman.

Emily gave her a puzzled look.

"The date," said Miss Linton, smiling. "You've forgotten the date, my dear."

35

O tried to remember the twists and turns they'd taken the day she went to the Linton house with Emily. But one street looked exactly like the next. The sun was setting, and lights were going on in the houses she passed. People were settling down after dinner, satisfied and sleepy at the end of a long day. The ghostly glow of TV screens flickered on the walls of rooms like cold fire.

And here she was, hurrying along these winding streets in search of a house different in kind from all the others. But where was it? She struggled to pierce the shroud of panic that had settled over her, to recall some street name, some landmark, something.

You're being ridiculous, the sensible voice in her head told her. This story is pure fiction. She wished Rimbaud was here with her now. For all his strangeness – and he was truly the strangest person she'd ever met – he would understand why she had to find this house, why the sight of the sun scraping the tops of the trees woke such terror in her.

If she didn't find the house before the dark settled in, she would have little chance of finding it at all. But she mustn't think like that, she told herself, as she hurried down yet another street. There was something familiar about this one – that house set back on the hill, the striped awnings over the windows.

And then she saw it – the duct-taped taillight, the faded STOP THE WAR sticker on the bumper. She stopped dead, and then approached the car slowly, as if it might scurry off like Psycho if it saw her. She peered in the window. Backseat strewn with papers, statue of the Virgin stuck to the dashboard, ashtray once again pulled into service. This was Emily's car, all right.

She straightened and looked down the street. Emily wasn't blind. She knew her car was – different. She would have parked it a little way from the Linton house and walked. Up ahead, a side street branched off. She ran up to it, and there it was – the little cul-de-sac she'd been searching for.

From the opposite end, the Linton house looked back at her. It was a creepy enough old house in the daylight. Now, in the dying light, it looked downright forbidding. She moved cautiously along the street, approaching the place as she might a strange dog. The neighboring house on this side of the street had disappeared. A slack plastic fence had been thrown up around the property across from it. The house-eating monster was sitting in that yard now, its iron jaws gaping, its dull sleep filled with dreams of broken brick and plaster, splintered wood and glass.

She stopped in front of the Linton house, suddenly full of doubt. The house looked empty. For a crazy moment, in the unsure light, she thought she saw boards in the upper windows, as if the building were deserted. Two large crows lifted off from a nearby tree in a sudden flurry of wings, making a slow circle in the sky. As they settled on the roof of the old house, the vision vanished, and she saw a dim light flickering in the turret room.

Taking a deep breath, she pushed open the gate and started up the walk. The ground felt uncertain under her, as if the pavement had heaved. She jumped as the gate slapped closed behind her.

She brought the heavy brass knocker down twice against the door and heard it echo inside. She waited, then rapped on the door again. Bending down, she lifted the flap on the mail slot and peered in at the empty hall and the dim staircase winding off to the upper floors.

Beside the porch, a bay window protruded from the front room of the house. She cupped her hands to the glass and looked in. Simultaneously, on the other side, a chalk-white face pressed against the glass and peered into her eyes. Gasping, she jumped back, then realized it was just her reflection. Hurrying off the porch, she headed down the driveway to the back of the house, with a sick feeling in the pit of her stomach.

The face in the window lingered a moment, looking out on the falling dark, then drifted from the glass and was swallowed up in the shadows of the room.

"You've forgotten the date," said Miss Linton.

Suddenly Emily realized she *had* forgotten – forgotten it was August 8. Her pen was poised over the paper. She could feel the old woman's eyes intent upon her. Thoughts raced helter-skelter through her mind. She could tear up the check, say she'd changed her mind, and leave the house immediately.

And achieve what? Throw away her chance to reap the rewards of years of work? Let go of an opportunity that comes once in a lifetime? She looked down at the books on the table and the surrounding shelves, then over at Miss Linton – and signed the date.

"Splendid. Then it's all settled."

"I think I'll pack up a few of these books now," said Emily. "My car is just around the corner. If you'll leave a key with me, I'll come back with a van to collect the rest tomorrow."

Miss Linton nodded. She stood watching as Emily packed the books on the table into one of the cardboard boxes, and then lit the way with the candle as they proceeded cautiously down the steep stairs and along the dim hall. The box of books was much heavier than Emily had imagined. She strained to keep hold of it.

The candle threw weird shadows on the wall as they descended the stairs to the ground floor. Halfway down, a sharp pain surged down Emily's left arm. Another hit her squarely in the chest. As it knifed through her, she thought, This is it. This is the big one. She cried out.

At the foot of the stairs, Lenora Linton slowly turned to face her. But, in the act of turning, she was transformed. It was as if her shadow had detached itself from the wall and taken on flesh. She grew and stretched. Her gray hair went dark as night. Her dress became a suit of black. And the face that swung to meet Emily's terrified gaze belonged to the figure that had haunted her dreams.

The magician smiled up at her. "*How good of you to come. The show is about to begin.*" There was no movement of his mouth, no exhalation of breath, but the words resounded inside her, as though they'd been whispered from the bottom of a well.

Pain seared through her chest, more pain than she had ever felt. She gasped, and the box slipped from her hands. Her hands flew to her chest, her legs folded under her, and she felt herself tumbling like a rag doll down the stairs.

36

*S*he fell endlessly – through space, through time. It was as though a bottomless pit had opened under her. And all the while, a soothing, insistent voice kept repeating in her head:

There's nothing to fear, my child. Nothing at all to fear.

Suddenly, she was no longer falling, neither had she landed. Instead, she lay suspended in the air. Her eyes were sealed as if she were asleep, but she was not. She could hear every word the magician spoke.

"And now, my friends, you can see that our volunteer has ascended from the platform and sleeps peacefully in the air. I will pass this hoop, like so, along the length of her body to prove there are no wires or other hidden devices holding her aloft. Nothing but magic holds her here."

A sound of excited applause echoed through the room.

"And now our gracious sleeper will once again descend to earth. On the count of three, she will awaken – and remember nothing."

She felt herself drift slowly down and come to rest on solid ground.

"One. Two. Three," said the magician and lightly clapped his hands. She opened her eyes and found herself lying on a makeshift stage in a large darkened room. A magician stood beside her, smiling. His face was pale, his lips red as blood, his eyes deep and mesmerizing. She seemed to know him somehow. He extended his hand and helped her to her feet.

Seated on the floor before the stage, their faces ghostly in the glow of the gaslight, a group of children clapped excitedly. They were dressed in the fashion of a century ago. She looked down at herself and saw that she was dressed in the same way, a child among children.

Panic washed over her. But the magician laid his hand gently on her arm, and instantly it passed. "Take a bow, young lady," he said.

She looked around the darkened room, dazed and disoriented, as if she had been wrenched from a deep sleep. Yes, she remembered now, she had been dreaming, and in the dream she had been carrying something. It had been very heavy – her arms still ached with it – and somehow she had stumbled and fallen.

But it had only been a dream. His hand resting on her arm was like her mother's, comforting her when some night terror woke her from sleep.

"The young lady may take her seat again," said the magician.

"And for her kind assistance, the professor will present her with a copy of his little book."

The book he handed her was achingly familiar. She stood looking down at it, knowing she had seen it at some other time, in some other place. She had the gnawing sense that some larger reality had slipped from her grasp.

They seemed to be in a room in a house, a large circular room that had been made over for a magic show. In the shadows, beyond the feeble reach of the gas lamps, she could see furniture pushed back against the wall. Her eyes lingered on a set of high-backed, red-velvet armchairs, ranged against the wall beside a large fireplace. She had the feeling she'd been in this room before.

"Well, then," said the magician, "since it seems the young lady wishes to remain onstage, perhaps we can enlist her aid with the final attraction of the evening." From the rear of the stage, he wheeled forward the large brazier of burning coals that had stood glowing in the shadows like a beating heart since the beginning of the show.

"Fire," he said as he passed his hand over the brazier. Flames leapt from the live coals. "Truly, it is one of life's great mysteries. So beautiful to behold; so dangerous to touch. The ancients believed the salamander could survive even in the midst of fire. And now, with the aid of magic, we shall do the same."

He suddenly plunged his hands into the brazier as if it were a basin of cool water. A gasp went up from the crowd. He picked up a glowing coal and popped it in his mouth, like a piece of candy. Turning to the awestruck audience, he plucked an oyster from the air and placed it on the coal in his mouth. It sizzled there for a few seconds and the shell opened. He reached in and took it out, along with the coal.

"I will ask my young assistant to prove to you that this oyster is cooked," he said as he handed it to her. The shell was hot. On his instructions, she scooped the meat from the oyster and ate it. It burned her throat a little as she swallowed.

The magician performed several more feats with the burning coals. "And now," he said, "we will bestow this same power on our young assistant here – the power to master fire. Come along, young lady, don't be shy."

But she didn't want to go to him. She could feel the heat of the fire against her face as she stood beside the flaming brazier.

"Come, come, my child. There's nothing to fear." His voice was soft and soothing, but hidden beneath it was another voice as fierce as fire.

Come to me, girl. I said, come.

He held his hand over the flaming coals as he extended it to her. It glowed red in the flames, yet remained miraculously unharmed. As she moved irresistibly toward him, she stumbled and looked down.

The floor was strewn with books. A shard of memory cut through the scene like a knife through a painted screen. She remembered an unbearable pain in her chest, remembered falling, books tumbling about her.

And then it was gone, and there was only the hushed room, the beckoning voice, the bottomless eyes. As she reached her hand out slowly to him, the sight of it sent a shock through her – for it was the thin, speckled hand of an old woman. For a moment, some shocking truth seemed about to dawn –

Then his flaming hand closed over hers and all thought fled. Like a tissue tossed in a fire, the room and everything in it hovered for an instant in space, then flared up and was gone. And there were only the two of them.

Flames enfolded every part of him. His clothes were woven flame, his hair a flaming torch, his flesh tongued with fire. He was Fire. The sweet hiss and crackle of his voice sounded in her head.

Come to me. We are one, you and I. There is no pain, nothing to fear.

He fixed her with his eyes; she could feel them searing into every part of her. He drew her slowly to him and enfolded her in his flaming arms. Such sweet pain pulsed through her that she thought she must die from it.

His breath was like the smell of roses on a summer night, but below lay the acrid smell of smoke and singeing hair, of smoldering cloth and wool.

Just a little sleep. A little sleep.

She felt herself spiraling helplessly down into the dark.

37

The sun hung red on the horizon as O came round to the back of the house. As she was climbing the porch stairs, she caught sight of a figure huddled by the door. She jumped back, and then realized it was just a pile of debris. Stepping past it, she pounded on the door. The sound died into the deep hush of the house.

Suddenly she smelled fire. She looked down and saw smoke drifting out lazily under the door. Cupping her hand to the window, she looked in. The dim room inside opened onto a long hall. The far end of the hall was lit by flames. For a moment she thought she saw two figures standing in their midst. But then there was only one.

"Emily!" she screamed as the figure slumped to the floor.

She plucked a loose brick from the pile of debris and smashed the glass in the door. Smoke streamed out into the night. She reached her arm through the ragged hole and groped for the handle. Her hand closed over what felt like a small chill hand, balled into a fist. She gave it a twist, and the door opened.

Dashing into the house, she ran for the hall. The smoke ran to meet her. It wrapped its arms around her, filling her lungs with its searing breath and blinding her eyes. She yanked her shirt up over her mouth and groped her way along the hall.

She hadn't gone far before dizziness and nausea overwhelmed her. She couldn't see, couldn't breathe. She no longer knew the way forward or the way back. In some impossibly calm corner of her, she thought, This is the part where you die. A dark hole seemed to open under her, and she tumbled in.

She found herself back at the Green Man, standing high on the shaky ladder outside the shop, staring into that ageless, knowing face. But the cracks had vanished, the flaking paint had fallen away, and life pulsed within the pale green flesh.

He swayed in the wind, and she swayed with him. She looked into his eyes, and he looked back. Instead of creaks, words came. He called her by name. And the vines that were his arms reached out and wrapped themselves around her. She was enfolded in them, lifted lightly up and carried.

Fresh air filled her burning lungs. She breathed in the rich dark smell of soil and leaf mold, felt the cool green dampness of the ravine against her skin as she was gently laid down.

And then there was nothing. . . .

When she woke, she was lying in the long grass in the backyard of the Linton house. A sickle moon shone down from a sky strewn with stars. Emily lay on the grass beside her, her face streaked with soot, her eyes shut. She looked ghostly pale in the moonlight, and for one terrifying moment, O thought she was dead. But then she saw the faint rise and fall of her chest.

How on earth did we get out of the house? she wondered dully, as she tried to piece together what had happened. The wail of sirens sounded in the distance.

The sirens grew steadily louder. Soon there were lights flashing and firefighters running about, smashing windows, training hoses on the burning house. A pair of ambulance attendants came hurrying into the yard with a stretcher. They lifted Emily onto it and wheeled her off to a waiting ambulance.

O turned and saw Rimbaud, striding from the shadows where the yard fell away into the ravine. He knelt beside her and took her hand in his. She tried to speak, but the effort brought on a fit of coughing.

"Shhh. Don't try to talk now," he said as he knelt by her side and assured her everything would be all right. She closed her eyes.

The attendants returned for her. As they were lifting her onto the stretcher, she asked, "Can he ride with me?" A strange look passed between them. When she turned to where Rimbaud had been, she found that he had vanished silently back into the shadows.

The firefighters were still training their hoses on the smoking building, when the attendants wheeled her around to the front of the house and lifted her into the back of the ambulance. One of them slipped an oxygen mask onto her face.

As she felt herself drifting off, she glanced out the ambulance window and imagined she saw Rimbaud standing there, as she had first seen him standing at the window of the Green Man.

38

They sat together in the car for a long while without saying a word, each lost in her own thoughts. Emily's bandaged arms rested on the steering wheel. Her fingers tapped out the beat of a slow tune by Bill Evans playing on the car stereo. Beside her, O sat looking out the window at the Linton house. She'd tried to talk Emily out of coming back here, but her aunt had insisted. She said something about needing to lay the ghost.

Two weeks had passed since the night of the fire. It had been a time of endless questions and few answers. The police had questioned them in the recovery room at the hospital on the night of the fire. What had Emily been doing at the house that night? How had the fire started? How had O managed to get her aunt out?

Emily insisted she'd been invited to the house by the owner, Lenora Linton, to buy a collection of books. They told her that was impossible. When she continued to insist, they passed her along to the hospital psychiatrist, who explained to her that the house had sat vacant for over a year – since the death of Lenora Linton. In the end, they put the entire matter down to a case of mild dementia and released her.

O had her own questions. She had been praised for rescuing her aunt from the fire that night. She didn't bother telling them she wasn't the one who had done the rescuing at all, but a mysterious third party no one else seemed to have seen – a boy without a name, who lived in a hut in a ravine. She figured it was enough for them to think just one of them was crazy.

The trouble was, she wasn't entirely convinced she *wasn't* crazy. After all, she, too, had seen this boarded-up shell of a house lived in and whole. She had sat sweating with Emily in front of the fire and spoken with Lenora Linton face-to-face. On the night of the fire, she had seen two figures standing in the flames at the end of the hall. Had she simply imagined it all? And had the smoke and flames so disoriented her that she only imagined Rimbaud there?

She hadn't told Emily anything about her trip to the ravine earlier that day, the discovery of the hut, her encounter with him there. Since the night of the fire, he had utterly vanished. And she wasn't about to go down into the ravine again, looking for him. She was afraid of what she might find.

She looked out the window of the car at the empty lot where the house that neighbored the Linton house had stood. With it gone, she could see the canopy of trees in the ravine that ran behind it. She was convinced it was the same ravine, snaking its way through Caledon, edging ever closer to the Linton house through the years, until finally it threatened to draw it down.

Emily opened the car door. "I'll be back in a few minutes," she said.

"Where are you going?"

"I'm going in there."

"Are you crazy?"

"Absolutely." And she stepped out of the car.

"Then I'm coming with you."

Emily leaned in through the window. "No, you're not, young lady. You're going to wait right here. This is something I have to do alone."

Despite the damage, the house was as remote and forbidding as ever. The front door had been scarred by ax blows. The heavy brass knocker dangled by a screw. Yellow police tape had been strung across the doorway like a web. Emily gave the door a push, and it edged open. She stooped under the tape and stepped inside.

The hall walls were blackened from the blaze. The acrid smell of charred wood and damp cinders hung in the air. But the floor seemed sound and the walls solid. She sensed no danger.

She stopped partway down the hall and pushed open the door on the left, into the large round room with the fireplace set against the far wall. The room was in ruins, the walls charred and broken, the lathing gaping through like bone. But she knew that, if she simply imagined hard enough, she could fill it in an instant with a makeshift stage, a group of excited children, the flickering glow of gas jets, and a magician with a deep melodious voice and eyes that burned into one's very soul.

Many years ago, when Lawrence Linton had lived in the house, another fire had occurred in this very room. Isaac Steiner had unearthed the story while looking into the Linton family's history. He had been by to visit them since the night of the accident and had shown them articles and photos from the newspapers of the time.

Apart from his work as an architect, Lawrence Linton had a fascination for the magical arts and took pride in being something of an amateur magician himself. Over time, he amassed a valuable collection of books on the subject.

He happened to meet a traveling magician who was passing through Caledon. In celebration of his niece's twelfth birthday, Linton arranged for the magician to give a special show to a group of children at the Linton house on the night of August 8.

During the show, something went terribly wrong. One of the illusions called for a brazier of burning coals. Somehow, it was overturned, and some of the stage trappings caught fire. Within minutes, the fire was out of control. In the general panic that followed, one child was left behind.

Linton never forgave himself. After that night, he was a changed man, plagued with guilt for the part he believed he had played in the tragedy. As time went by, he grew increasingly reclusive. He developed a peculiar obsession, which he committed to the pages of his private journal. He became convinced that the magician was more than mortal, and that the fire had been no accident. He confided to the journal that during the height of the blaze, when he ran back into the house in an attempt to rescue the child, he had seen the magician standing in the midst of the flames unharmed. After the fire, no trace of him was found, apart from a charred jacket draped over what seemed to be the blackened remains of a large rosebush.

Much of the latter part of Linton's journal was given over to his vain attempts to track down a traveling magician by name of Professor Mephisto. The name echoed eerily through the empty house now as Emily turned from the room and continued along the hall. She sensed that the magician was somehow still here, as present as the smell of smoke and cinders in the air.

She thought of O sitting in the car and of their conversation the night before. "If Lenora Linton died a year ago, who was it that called the shop, that showed us the collection, that was there with you on the night of the fire?"

"It was the magician. He is a master of illusion. He took that shape to serve his end."

And everything they had seen in the house had been an elaborate illusion, an intricate web spun by the spider to ensnare the fly. He had come for her this time, and had it not been for O, he would have succeeded.

She felt a chill run through her. For a moment, the house seemed to flicker like a flame. It slept now, but she felt the life pulsing through it still and knew it could transform in an instant. Her every instinct told her to flee the place – now – but she forced her feet to keep moving along the hall.

She paused at the foot of the winding stair, where O had seen her collapse on the night of the fire. The carved dragon coiled atop the newel post slept beneath a shroud of soot, unharmed. She had the feeling that the whole house might have burned down and it would still have survived. Sifting through the charred refuse on the floor with the toe of her shoe, she searched for some evidence of the books she had been carrying down the stairs that night. Something to prove she was not simply mad, as most everyone seemed inclined to believe.

But any books that might have spilled to the foot of the stairs had been consumed by the fire. She stood looking into the shadows of the upper floor, knowing she had to go up there, but wishing she were anywhere else in the world but here. The stairs had been badly damaged in the blaze, but when she put her weight on the charred boards, they seemed sound. She kept close to the side and started up.

Though the fire had not reached the second floor, the pervasive smell of smoke and cinders hung in the air. She moved cautiously along the hall, edging open one door after another, apprehension knotting her stomach into a tight ball.

Each room presented the same sad face. Desolation – the floors thick with dust, the walls bare, a few abandoned sticks of furniture scattered about. Sad remnants of the lives once lived here. There were signs of intruders as well – a ragged mattress in the corner of a room, empty beer and wine bottles, graffiti scrawled on the walls. All of it irrefutable proof that the place had sat empty for some time.

It should perhaps have given her some comfort, but it didn't. Instead, it gave her a dreadful sense of the creature's power. That all the elaborate trappings she had seen had been spun from – what? Imagination, desire, dream?

She remembered the uncanny sense she had when she first saw the inside of the house – that everything was just as she had imagined it would be. Somehow, it was the very strength of her own imagining that had helped bring the illusion to birth. And someone else would have conjured something else, after their own image.

It was desire that had brought her here, then as now. Then, it had been the desire to possess the impossible. Now, it was the desire to convince herself it was over, finished, done.

Yet was it ever really over? Three times in her life, the dark had come to her – in adolescence, in middle age, and now in old age. And each time, the collision with it had sent her careening off in a different direction. It had wounded her, yes, but at the same time it had deepened her resolve to survive, to create. Without it, she was convinced she would never have written a word. She would be someone else, living some other life. Would she be happy? Perhaps. But she would not be herself. She would not be Emily.

And now it would be up to another to watch and wait for the show's return.

She moved along the hall as if in a dream. At the foot of the stairs leading to the turret room, she stopped. Outdoors, it was midday, but here the shadows hung as if it were their home. She had pursued the nightmare through the house. There was no choice now but to follow it up these narrow stairs.

She went up slowly, pausing an eternity on each step. At last she stood in the dark at the top of the stairs. She put her ear to the door and listened, then turned the handle and stepped into the room.

She wasn't sure what she'd been expecting. Perhaps, in some secret part of her, she'd harbored the hope that the treasure she'd come so close to possessing would still be here, sublimely spared. What she found instead was the broken shell of a room. Several of the windows had been shattered. Broken glass splintered underfoot as she edged cautiously across the floor.

Pigeons had gained entrance through the broken windows and built their nests on the empty shelves. The floor beneath was spattered with droppings. Some of the nests were empty, but others still held birds. Agitated at the entrance of an intruder, they fluttered their wings and paced nervously up and down the shelves, eyeing her with their sideways gaze. With a loud beating of wings, several took flight and made their escape through the broken windows.

So these were the shelves where she had pored over the priceless volumes from the Linton collection. And this fireplace, choked with rubbish and dead leaves, was where she had dozed and dreamt in front of the fire.

She knew that if she curled up on the cold floor in front of it now and fell asleep, she would waken to the crackle of flames and the creak of Miss Linton's footsteps on the stairs. And the books would grace the shelves again and be spread in all their glory across the table. She was not mad. She had *not* simply imagined it. It *had* been here.

She took her bag from under her arm, opened it, and took out the book. It was an old, crudely produced, little book in paper wraps – the book she had slipped unknowingly into her bag that night. As she held it in her hand now, the room rippled for a second, like a painted scene. She sensed something moving just the other side of it. She could feel the stir of magic in the air, like the seductive scent of perfume.

Things hovered on the verge of visibility – all the former trappings of the room, the house, and its ghostly inhabitant. She could hear her name being called, the sound of footsteps in the shadows of the empty house as it slowly woke around her.

The book had turned brittle since it first found its way into her purse. In the beginning, she'd been tempted to slip it into a protective cover and place it among her collection. But each night it was in her possession, he had come to her in her dreams. She knew she must end it.

"Here," she said to the empty room, to the pigeons pacing the shelves, to the shattered windows and the cold, leaf-choked fireplace. "I'm done with it. I want none of it. It's yours. Do you hear me?"

And she tore the brittle pages into small pieces and let them flutter to the floor, where they shriveled, shrank, and crumbled into dust.

She heard footsteps coming slowly, steadily up the stairs. The door edged open – and O peeked her head around it. When she saw Emily standing dead still in the midst of the ruined room, she let out a shriek.

"Oh my God, you nearly gave me a heart attack," she said, throwing her hand up to her chest.

"And you me," said Emily.

"I've been calling and calling. You were gone so long, I got worried." She looked around the room, glancing nervously up at the pigeons, at the shattered windows and the glass-strewn floor. "Maybe we should go now," she said.

"Yes," said Emily. "We should go."

She took one last look around the room, then turned and followed O down the stairs.

39

The trouble with poets was that most of them happened to be crazy. Either they started out that way or they wound up that way in the end. It was what you might call an occupational hazard.

There were plenty of poets milling around the Green Man at that moment. Leonard Wellman had contacted several people from Emily's past to let them know about this special meeting of the Tuesdays at the Green Man. It was something of an anniversary, and he had an important announcement to make.

Emily was holding court in the back room, the object of attention of all who entered. Friends and fellow poets she hadn't seen in years had come. Gigi had kindly donated cookies for the occasion. O set them out on a tray, with a note reading *Compliments of Gigi's Patisserie* and a pile of Gigi's funky pink business cards alongside.

As O bustled around, setting up extra chairs and starting a second pot of coffee, her eyes kept drifting to the door. Despite the large turnout, there was no trace of the one person she really hoped would come. In honor of the occasion, she had agreed to read a couple of her poems, and she desperately wanted Rimbaud to be there to hear them.

Who knew where poems came from? In the end, they were a gift. All you could do was accept it with gratitude and carry it into the light as best you could. She was glad for what she'd been given and hoped she'd be given more. If nothing else, this incredible summer had taught her one thing – she was happiest at those times when words stirred inside her.

The Green Man was a place where extraordinary things happened. Not the least of those things had been meeting the mysterious stranger who had come into her life here. As she fingered the little amulet around her neck, she remembered what Isaac Steiner had said: it was a charm worn to ward off evil by invoking the names of guardian spirits.

In a way, that was what Rimbaud had been – her guardian spirit, watching over her in the night, catching her when she fell, rescuing her from danger. Well, she needed watching over now. So where was he?

Her eyes went to the door again. Night was falling, and the shop had begun to fill with shadows. She glanced over at Emily, who gave her a little nod to let her know they were ready to begin. That was her cue to go and lock the door. As she passed the poetry section, she imagined Rimbaud standing there, as she had seen him standing many times before. But he wasn't there, nor was he at the door. She looked up and down the empty street, then closed the door and hung the PLEASE KNOCK FOR POETRY READING sign in the window.

She settled herself on a chair inside the entrance to the reading room, where she could keep an eye open for latecomers. Emily rang the little brass bell to call the meeting to order, then rose from her seat and went to the front to address the gathering.

"To begin with, I'd like to thank you all for coming. I'm very happy to be here with you. As some of you may already know, the past few months have been something of a trial by fire for our little group. And, as you can see, I have not escaped entirely unscathed." She held up her bandaged arms, eliciting some quiet, uncomfortable laughter. "But I'm pleased to tell you tonight that those troubles appear to be over. My good friend and fellow poet Leonard Wellman has some exciting news he would like to share."

Leonard came up and stood beside her. "Good evening. It's great to see such a large turnout. I'm glad you could come. I think I echo everyone's sentiments when I say how delighted I am that the Tuesdays have resumed. For a good many years now, these meetings have been a source of support and inspiration for poets young and old and for all who value poetry.

"As a young man fresh out of school with a passion for writing poetry, I can well remember feeling I was some freak of nature, alone in the world. The Tuesdays have shown me that we are not alone, or if we are, we are alone together.

"Some months back, when the continued existence of our little group seemed to hang in the balance, I approached the local arts council with a request for an operating grant. I'm pleased to announce tonight that the Caledon Arts Council has awarded us that grant. And so, for the foreseeable future at least, the wolf is no longer at the door. And the Tuesdays at the Green Man will go on."

There was heartfelt applause. Leonard gave Emily a kiss on the cheek and returned to his seat. Emily smiled down at her hands in her shy way and waited for the applause to die down.

"It is somehow fitting that this wonderful news should come to us now," she said. "For it was twenty-five years ago this month that Leonard and I and a small group of others initiated these readings. None of us at the time ever dreamt they would continue this long.

"Styles have changed over the years. Voices have changed. But many things remain the same. Writing is a lonely business, and writing poetry is perhaps the loneliest kind of writing. No one gets rich writing poetry. But that's not the reason one does it.

"You write because you must – because, for whatever reason, you have fallen in love with words – with the taste of them on the tongue, the feel of them flowing through the pen, the sight of them on the page. And as long as this world retains its mystery and wonder, there will be those who continue to fall beneath the spell.

"I have grown old in this work, but the spirit leaps in me still. If we are to keep the spirit of poetry strong, there must be new voices to come and take up the task, poets who bring their youth, their passion, and their vision to this age-old craft. Poetry is many things, but above all else, it is the constantly renewed vision of hope. To that end, I am pleased to present to you tonight a young woman ready to take up the torch. I give you – Ophelia Endicott."

Right up until Emily said her name, O had been searching the room for the young new voice Emily was going on about. Now, as applause filled the air and heads turned to her, she felt her heart pound and her cheeks burn. Gathering her manuscript from where she'd tucked it on a nearby shelf, she made her way to the stage. She set the sheets down on the podium and glanced nervously over the group.

"Thank you," she said. "When I told my aunt I might read tonight, she failed to mention that she might call me up first. I'll have to talk to her about that a little later. I have a couple of things I'd like to share with you. Both were written this summer and both, I suppose, are about poetry."

She cleared her throat, took a deep breath, and began to read the "Garden Sculpture" poem. When she finished, she glanced apprehensively down at the audience. There was Emily, beaming up at her. Beside her, Leonard Wellman was giving her the thumbs-up sign. Miles was there as well, and beside him Gigi was sitting with Tiny from the Mind Spider – both, in their own way, poets themselves. For wherever something was done with grace and beauty, there was poetry.

Sitting sedately to the side was Isaac Steiner, who'd been such a help in the difficult weeks following the fire. He had witnessed with them the remarkable change that the carriage-house books had undergone during that time. The smell of mildew and damp that had seeped deep into them, and which nothing they did seemed able to remove, had mysteriously faded. Rippled pages had flattened, and the foxy brown spots that marred many of the books had disappeared. It was as though they'd been under a spell that had suddenly been lifted. Emily decided to donate several of the miraculously restored volumes to the university for Dr. Steiner's research. She was adding the remainder to her private collection as a nest egg against whatever surprises the future might send her way.

The room was full, but there were guests the others couldn't see. Tucked in a corner at the back, Mallarmé was smoking one of his delicate French cigarettes. Pound was stroking his beard and staring intently at the ceiling. Miss Dickinson was nestled quietly in the shadows, the whisper of a smile on her face.

O's eye drifted to the doorway. And there stood Rimbaud, leaning against the door frame, looking at her through those dark heavy-lidded eyes of his. His hands were pushed deep into his pockets, and his hair was rumpled. He gave her that crooked little grin, and something inside her melted. Emily followed her gaze and saw him standing there too. She turned to O and gave her a nod to let her know they were waiting for her to read her second poem.

"Thank you very much," said O. "Now the title of this next poem will, I'm sure, have a familiar ring to it. It's called 'The Green Man.'"

Up until then, she had been reading from the sheet, afraid the words would slip from her mind as she stood on the stage. But as she started up again now, she recited the poem purely from memory. The words came slow and sure. She lingered over each before she let it go. There were plenty of people in the room, but this was meant especially for one.

"When first I saw you
Suspended above the oblivious street,
Your weatherworn face, your words
Reduced to rusty squeaks,
Speech seemed something that eluded you.
The vines that spilled
From the margins of your mouth
Wound about you, bound you.
I longed to lop them away
And free you . . ."

In a week's time, she'd be heading back home. She wanted Rimbaud to promise he'd write to her, send her gifts of poems on pale blue paper. She wanted to say she'd be back at the Green Man next summer and hoped he would be too. All she had for now were the words of the poem, but she sensed he could hear those other thoughts as clearly as if she'd whispered them in his ear.

". . . It was only later I learned
You spoke in ways
I failed to understand.
I lacked the glossary for leaves
And branches, the lexicon for life
That roots itself in mystery
And reaches for the light."

When she'd first arrived at the Green Man, she would never have imagined herself standing here, reading her work. But from the moment she stepped through the door, she'd sensed this was a place of magic. It had worked its magic on her. She was not the person she had been. She had joined the ranks of those crazy people who call themselves poets.

It was her business now to believe – in the power and beauty of words, in the spirits that move among us always, in the worlds of light and dark that neighbor us – to believe in the possibility of the impossible.

Outside the shop, the Green Man swayed in time to the words of the poem. The vines that sprang from his mouth curled and wound about his head. The carved leaves fluttered lightly in the breeze. One of the birds that sheltered among the branches opened its beak in song.

The End.